Beyond Love

Beyond Love

What lies beneath?

Ankit Uttam

MAHAVEER PUBLISHERS

Published by

MAHAVEER PUBLISHERS

4764/2A, 23-Ansari Road, Daryaganj

New Delhi – 110002

Ph. : 011 – 66629669–79–89

Fax : 011 – 41563419

e-mail : mahaveerpublishers@gmail.com

First Published: August 2010

Beyond Love

ISBN (10) : 818352012X

ISBN (13) : 9788183520126

Distributed by

VAIBHAV BOOK SERVICE

e-mail : vaibhavbookservice@gmail.com

Published by D.K. Jha for Mahaveer Publishers

Printed by Jaico Printers, New Delhi

Dedications

To my Mummy, Papa, brother Kalpit who supported me by being so unsupportive in every field except when he had to take some space in the acknowledgments section

and,

last but never the least,
my only saviour when I was depressed or deviated from my goals when the path was filled with darkness – the love of my life, Moti.

Acknowledgement

A book is written by the author but the final product, which you are holding right now in your hands, is the result of many people. To start with, for my Oscar-night speech, I would like to express my gratefulness to all my mentors who knowingly or unknowingly mentored me by their actions, words or their books. I would not have been what I am today without the support of books and words of wisdom of Ayn Rand, Earl Nightingale, Robert Kiyosaki, Zig Ziglar, Chetan Bhagat and above all, God.

{Applause}

The next list consists of my parents, my brother Kalpit and my life support system, Nishu.

{Applause continues.........}

Another list contains the following names, but before I announce the names, I would like to request you to please bear with me. I promise I won't take much of your time. So here are the names of those who gave their support through this journey:

Dhawan, my partner Aditi, Sonal Moti, Roma, Ashwani, Ankur, Phaatak, Avinash, Shuchi, Chimpu, Smita, Maindy, Deepak, Vishal, Shobhit, Rastogi, Vijay (man, I am loving this section the most), Sneha ma'am, Gaurav sir, Nitin, Anugrah, Winnie, Aarti, Sandra, Ramandeep, Pawan Sir, Sapna Didi, Shubhangi, my luckiest shishya and Aman Gupta. Dude wherever you are, I know you are watching all of us. Guys and gals, without your support, this book would not have taken shape.

{More applause}

Now, coming to the last set of the names, I would like to thank Mahaveer Publishers for giving me this opportunity to show my disabilities to the world; Mr Azeem for taking my numerous calls without any sign of irritation and Mr Dilip for spending his time in explaining the whole process of publishing a book.

Well, that's all. If any of the names have been left out in this section, don't forget to remind me by sending me an e-mail at ankit.uttam@gmail.com. You can also send your comments, thoughts or any questions you may have in mind to the same id.

A Remembrance

Remembering my classmates, after a few years,
filled my eyes with tears.
Everyone now is a busy lot,
no one can escape destiny's plot.

Saw the girl whom once I thought was my best friend,
oops! Today she is somebody else's girl friend.
After months, remembered her for a little while,
heard she is happy; that made me smile.

Project reviews to campus interviews,
nick-names to last-bench games.
Cultural rehearsals to love proposals,
short-term crusades to classroom blushes.

Everything is fresh in our mind,
only wish life could just rewind.
Let's laugh, play and rejoice,
once again become college-guys.

Chatting and laughing, we all were in elation,
till the painful moment of separation.
When it was time to part,
we returned with a heavy heart.

Today life is full of commitments,
and too many worries.
But those cherished moments,
will live forever in our memories.

Source: Internet

Prologue

Trin…nng! Trin…nng! The phone rang bitterly, conveniently squashing my thoughts. But I chose to stay where I was, watching the TV.

'Anshul, pick up the phone,' Mom cried from the kitchen.

I made no attempt to move from my place.

'Oh my God, this boy,' finally Mom had to come. She glared at me. I avoided her icy gaze with the newspaper in front.

'Hello! Yes, Anshul is here. Who is speaking?'

'Must be Aayush,' I thought.

'Udita! Are you Anshul's classmate?' Mom's questions were like a never-ending train.

'Udita!' I sprang into action. 'Mom, give me the phone,' said I, literally snatching the receiver from her hand. She threw me a quizzical look while handing over the receiver to me.

'What will happen to you? Only girls call you. Don't you have any guy as a friend?' Mom left with her usual parting shot.

'Yeah, Udita, what happened? Why are you crying?' I was shocked to hear her sobbing on the phone.

'Bhaiya, Mom and Di have met with an accident while coming from Nanaji's house today. Both are injured but Di is very serious,' she kept on crying.

I felt a knife cutting through my flesh with every passing

moment. 'It can't be true; it is just a nightmare,' I thought. 'It can't be true. This simply can't happen.'

I remained standing near the phone long after the call was over, hoping against hope that someone would tell me that it was all a bad joke and that nothing had happened.

I felt a hand on my shoulder. I turned around to see Mom's eyes fixed on me.

'Mom, I have to go. I will explain to you everything later. There is a train from Lucknow at 10:30 in the night.'

1

In Deep Pit

'You are a failure, a complete failure.'

'Your life is now finished.'

'You cannot do anything in your life, Bro.'

'You are good for nothing, mate.'

'We are ashamed of you, son.'

It all started with a mistake – the mistake which I had committed at the age of eighteen.

Results of IIT-JEE screenings, AI-EEE and UPSEE were out and so were the one-liners followed by a dismayed look on the faces of my well-wishers, with all kinds of questions floating in their eyes about my gloomy future.

It might not be tough for you to guess that I had been badly battered in the race for scoring a good rank in the competitive exams. I had even wasted a year in the city close to my home on attending coaching classes in the company of my two friends, Ankush and Ashmit.

Ankush cracked IIT-JEE and got Electronics and

Communication Trade at the IIT, Delhi and Ashmit, although unable to clear the IIT mains, finally got Electrical Engineering in a government college of Uttar Pradesh Technical University. Also, the icing on the cake was Rashmi, who was one of my classmates pursuing her B.Sc from Benaras Hindu University. She appeared for the exams and got Computer Science in the same college as Ashmit.

I was quite relaxed about my results, the reason being the amount of hard work that I had put into my studies, *until* I came to know the resuits of others. I knew that my marks were merely a reflection of my dislike for mathematics, which is an indispensable part of engineering entrance exams. However, I was not able to control myself from feeling bad about it; in reality, it infuriated me considerably.

Feelings are solely relative – that was the day when I really understood this reality in full measure.

My parents were completely devastated at my results and stopped talking to me in a normal human voice. Mum's mood vacillated as per the mood of Papa and on observing his expressions, I felt like an unwanted piece of filth at home. The atmosphere in the house was rather grim. Even in the month of June I felt an unnerving chill in my room, as if my house had shifted to Alaska. I felt as though nobody wanted to see me and I slowly confined my activities to the four walls of my small room. I didn't want to see anyone's face – face with eyes; eyes with pity for me; eyes showing shame for me; eyes revealing disappointment at me; and eyes having anger for me.

I was only waiting for the college selections to take place as only then could I assess how cramped my situation was and what I had to do to get out of it. I knew that my low rank wouldn't be able to get me admission in any good college, but I decided to hang around and wait for my fate to unravel its mystery. Finally, after a long wait, which appeared as if it was stretching for years, the day arrived.

I reached the counselling centre at around 9:30 a.m. and after document verification, I was directed towards a room where I had to attend to an age-old computer. While I was filling my options, my legs began to tremble, reminding me of the presence of my bones. Something inside my head screamed that the computer could crash mid-way and if not, then the invigilator would definitely come to me and say, 'Sorry, but you didn't get admission in any of the colleges. Try next year.'

I tried to get my breathing right, but this became possible only after I had locked all my choices and obtained a hard copy of it as proof. It was only the next day that I got to know the name of the college in which I had secured admission. At last, I could study Computer Science at Girdhari Lal Smarak College of Engineering & Technology, Bareilly.

I was relatively happy because now my days at home were limited and at least I had a vague idea what lay in store for me. Papa wanted me to opt for Electronics and Communication as my first choice, but finally I got the subject of my choice. Now I only had to wait; so I was waiting.

2

The Eye-opener

Twelfth September was the date when we, that is, Father and I, boarded the train for Bareilly. My former classmate Afzal was already studying there and he had joined it just after school. This way he had no coaching to take or suffer any heartache. But now the equations had changed. He was my senior and I was his not-so-worthy junior.

On reaching the Bareilly railway station, we went straight to meet my only saviour there. So far I had been rather sceptic about the college environment and most importantly, about the ragging. I had dreamed that my college would be something like the college seen in the movie '*Kuch Kuch Hota Hai*' with cool professors teaching luvology, handsome dudes playing guitars and the prettiest of girls dancing around and that too, many of them, but after meeting him, I got to know what I could expect. He was all praise for the college, its atmosphere, its discipline and most importantly, its devotion towards academics. Aghh!

But all his sentences of praise soon vanished when I was

left alone with him. Then he came out with the real story, blow by blow.

'Look Anshul, now that you have got admission here, I want to give you a true picture by unveilling the truth,' Afzal said in a hushed voice, clearly afraid of being overheard by my father.

'The real thing? What you had told so far was some kind of a fairytale? What are you talking about?' I asked in an angry tone.

'Well, what I told Uncle was not the complete truth. The truth is very different to what I said.'

'Look Afzal, I know that you know that you are my senior now, but this is no time for ragging,' I tried to be curt with him, thinking that he was playing some kind of a joke on me.

'Anshul, I am not kidding. Actually when you asked me about the college on the phone and what I said today is correct but only on the surface. Deep down it is not as simple as it seems. Actually, I don't know how to frame it.'

'Afzal, why are you mystifying this whole thing? Just tell me what you have in mind,' said I, rather irritated at his prolonged speech.

'Anshul, what I told you about discipline is actually superficially true. You see, discipline and strictness are two different things. Discipline comes from within, but strictness is imposed; and here it is imposed much too severely.'

'You mean to say that this is more school-like?'

'Hey, don't compare it with the school. The school was a far better place. The word 'jail' would be appropriate to be used here,' he said warningly, 'and the jailor here is the MD of this college,' he completed the statement.

'You mean he is a kind of Hitler or something?' I asked.

'Well, as a matter of fact, I have only read about Hitler and that is not much. But I think if he would have been alive, then our MD would have been his favourite commander.'

I gave a reluctant laugh.

'As I had told you, mobile phones are not allowed in the college premises,' Afzal continued.

'That, I think, is a good thing. Using mobiles during lectures should be banned,' I said pompously.

'Now you also know that the hostels are also a part of the college premises.'

'Yes I know that…W...h…a…t t…h…e…e…?' I screamed, horror-struck at the mere realisation. 'Now this can't be true! You surely must be joking. *Aren't you*?'

'No, my dear, no,' he assured me in a saint-like voice. 'It is a fact that mobiles are strictly prohibited in the college campus and in the hostel,' he said, as if reading from some notice-board.

'Dude, this is the 21st century and without mobiles, life is simply impossible,' I continued.

'Well, then start practising now because this is not the end; it is ony the tip of the iceberg. Now you will begin your new life and also one more thing, 'co-roaming' is a strict 'no' here, else you will be fined heavily.'

'What? You mean we not only can't ogle at the ice-cream, but can't touch it or have it too.' This was indeed the limit. College life without girls is like a wardrobe without a pair of jeans, a pressure cooker without its whistle and a mobile without a sim card. 'How are you all surviving here?' I asked, really pissed off at it all.

'Well dude, rules are meant to be broken and here

everyday new rules are imposed on us. But in a few days' time, everything gets back to as it's before and the best way to avoid any problem is to remain unnoticed in this crowd. If you try to act smart, there are many in the waiting, longing to outsmart you. And in this jail, acads are everything. So be devoted to your studies.'

'But I thought college means life minus studies,' I said, as it was hard for me to imagine Shahrukh Khan bumping his head agaist those thick, dusty books in the movies.

'So now it's high time that you change your definitions and I know you can do it,' said Afzal, smirking stupidly.

'Is there anything else which is remotely related to my survival in this jail?' I asked disdainfully. I was realising that my life was now completely screwed and that too due to this moron standing in front of me. If only he had given some hint about these things before the counselling, he would not have been able to display the broadest possible smile which I desperately wanted to wipe out from his face.

'Well the *fachchas*, I mean the first-year students, have to follow some simple rules till the fresher's party, if they want to survive in one piece,' he said disdainfully.

'And what are those simple rules?' I asked, sounding visibly rude.

'Firstly, the hair must be cut as close to the scalp as possible so as to deter the seniors from grabbing them with their angelic hands. Always follow the dress code from morning till you sleep at night; this means non-pleated trousers and a full-sleeved shirt. Belts and wrist-watches are not allowed. Anything and everything kept in the shirt's pocket will belong to the seniors ultimately. Wish every senior you meet and don't ever smile in front of them.

Always look at the third button of your shirt as you are not allowed to look at the faces of your seniors. Don't ask any questions and do not feel bad if we, the seniors, grab your collar and scold you for any damn thing because everything here is technical; nothing is personal.'

'Wow, what a holy feeling I am getting right now!'

'So, let's go.'

'Where?'

'For your hair-cut, dear.'

This way my not-so-long mane was peeled off and it was brutally ensured that I didn't bother my comb for at least the next two months.

* * * * *

I found myself in the hostel at the mercy of some guards and our saviour, the warden.

The first- and the second-year students lived in the same hostel with shutters dividing it into two parts. We rarely crossed the *Laxman rekha* of our junior lobby and if anyone wanted to go to the PCO or anywhere outside, then first of all he had to find some guy with the same aspirations and then move in a line because that was the only way allowed in public.

The first day of college was the orientation day and I was really impressed with the concept on hearing of it. We all were instructed to gather in the auditorium to attend it. That was the first time when I was out in the open, in the midst of so many predators. I was very careful not to remain at any of the extreme ends of the line. I very carefully chose to be in the middle of it, so as to enjoy the best of both worlds. Although we were not allowed to look at any of our seniors' faces, our only option was to look at the tiles, but that confounded our problem of finding our way to the auditorium. Finally, after eighteen minutes, we were able to stumble through our way to the auditorium.

My mind was filled with all kinds of thoughts about the orientation programme, but on entering the auditorium, my first expression was, 'What the f*** is this place?' I saw that the expression was nearly the same in each pair of eyes following me. The room in which we entered was nowhere near the standards of an auditorium. It was simply a small room with a bump at one end, which could be called a dais for one's satisfaction.

Soon the programme began. After a speech by the chairman, our future professors, one by one, started coming on to the dais to tell us something related to our future. It was no easy task to concentrate upon what was being said as most of us were half dozing. Finally the speech session got over and we were taken for a round of our prospective home for the next four years. I only remember looking at the design of the floor tiles while moving here and there in a queue. I felt as though I was a lamb let free among a bunch of tigers and lions, each waiting eagerly to pounce upon me. The only thing I remember doing was constantly repeating, "Good morning, sir!" In that time, the uppermost desire in my heart was to run from there and seek the shelter of my room.

Soon my wish was fulfilled and I found myself in the safe confines of my room.

My first day had passed off peacefully. I was still alive, thought I, as I thanked my stars.

3

Ground Reality

A black hooded figure was chasing me as I was running for my life. It was a lonely place with bushes all around. Large trees were all over the place, blocking the sunlight. Not even a single ray was able to reach the ground. Suddenly my leg was hit with a stone and I fell down with a loud thump. I found the figure drawing nearer to me. I tried to get up, but he clasped my foot and started to pull me on the rough terrain. I tried to scream but my lips were tightly sealed, out of fear. Suddenly my hand found a stone and I threw it at the figure with all my might; but it didn't let go of me. I kept on hitting on his hands but he wouldn't let go, though he kept screaming with pain. The sound emanating from his mouth was very unusual – it sounded like the alarm clock. I woke up, deeply startled. The alarm tone was ringing loudly. It was 7 o'clock. I felt as if something heavy had been lifted off my chest. My roommates had still not arrived. So it was only me in the three-seater room. I sat on the bed, still reeling under the impact of my dream and an unusual fear gripped my mind.

The pleasant weather soon revived the mood of the air. I dressed myself and went for breakfast. It was 7:45 a.m. when I saw the boys making a beeline towards the lobby, even before the second-year students had completed their breakfast.

Though it was a bit early, it was comfortable to be in the classroom rather than being among my predators. Soon I was in my class, sitting with my head bent. Though there were no seniors in the class, I was really looking more than pathetic. Unfortunately, my college was a co-ed.

* * * * *

It was time for the first lecture when a professor entered the class and introduced himself as B.P. Saxena.

'Good morning!' he said.

'Go…oo…oo…od mo…oo…oo…rning, sir,' we all sang.

'I am B.P. Saxena and I'll teach you "Strength of Materials (SOM)". Is this clear? It is part of a very difficult subject in the first year of Mechanical Engineering. The other topic is thermodynamics and mechanics. Is it clear? Every year many students get their back burned in this paper. I mean, get through the paper by their sheer intelligence and I know that in your class also, there will be many like them. But I want you all to work hard so that you can avoid such an eventuality. Is that clear? I am telling you all this because getting good marks in this subject is like a mere dream. Is it clear?'

I didn't like him very much but found myself nodding my head endlessly at his every '*is it clear?*'

After his introduction, he talked about wedges, balances

and trusses interspersed with *'is it clear?'* Though I had understood literally nothing, but it was clear within a few minutes that the first three rows had to nod their heads more often than the others.

The next lecture was in Engineering Mathematics. It was the same subject that I loved to loathe and I cursed my luck that I had to study it here also. Soon enough, I found myself feeling drowsy. I sat with my eyes closed, pretending to be non-existent when suddenly a shrill voice pierced my ears. I opened my eyes in astonishment.

Oh my God, is this Maths? No, it can't be. It can't be true. Is it real? But what if it is real? No, it can't be real. I was looking with my eyes wide open.

'Good morning, students.'

'Good morning, ma'am.'

I found myself staring at the voice and this was the case with every silly guy in the class. She was wearing a cream chiffon sari that seemed to be made just for her. She had the most serene looking face that one sees only in one's dream. Her makeup was perfect; neither too light nor too loud. Her nose was pointed and separated two large eyes. What specially complimented her looks was her long hair that was tied delicately behind her back.

'I am Barkha Mishra and I will teach you Engineering Mathematics,' she announced while walking into the room as if it taking a walk in the garden or something.

That day, after the lecture was over, I knew I was going to love Maths and it marked the beginning of my affair with Maths.

The third lecture was in thermodynamics. A fragile-looking, partially-haired personality slithered into the room, introducing himself as Girish Katiyar. His behaviour suggested that his inclination was more towards the females in our class. I felt a negative vibe stretching itself throughout the room as if it was emanating from his body. Maybe I was prejudiced because his inclination towards the fair sex was obvious and that plagued my impression about him.

It was only 11:10 a.m., but pangs of hunger had already started troubling my stomach like never before. There were still two lectures to go before the lunch break. The fourth lecture was a free period and all of us started acquainting ourselves with our immediate and not-so immediate neighbours. I was amazed to see how easily some boys could interact with strangers. I found Akshay, a tall and sturdy-looking boy sitting next to me, talking animatedly to the girl sitting on the second bench. I was admiring his glib talk when Ravi, the other boy sitting with me, asked, 'So, are you from Bareilly?'

'No.'

'So, you must be a hosteller?'

How intelligent you are! I thought. 'You guessed it right,' I said

'Who is this guy?' he asked about Akshay.

'I don't know exactly, but I think his name is Akshay.'

'What does he think of himself? A stud?'

'Why? Why do you think so?' I smiled.

'See, how he is talking to that girl.'

'So, what's the problem? Is there something wrong?' I asked, somewhat peeved at his dog-in-the-manger attitude.

'I already have a girlfriend,' he said with pride in his voice.

Now what did that mean? I thought. 'Congratulations! Is she in this college?' I asked, suppressing my smile.

'No, she is my neighbour.'

'Sorry, I couldn't follow. Is she in school?' I asked, confused at his monosylabillic answer.

'Yeah, she is. But, talking like that won't impress that girl. I think that girl is desperate to get a boyfriend,' he said, glaring in Akshay's direction.

'I don't think so. You are passing your verdict too soon,' I said in a slightly dark tone.

'You don't know anything about these girls. Actually...'

'Good afternoon,' echoed a husky voice in the classroom. Each of us turned to locate its source and saw a fat-bellied, fair-complexioned gentleman standing behind us in the classroom. The fifth lecture started rolling. I let out a sigh of relief to be spared from hearing any more of the odious comments from Ravi.

'I am your Physics teacher and I'll also teach you basic Electronics. Since today is your first lecture, let's get acquainted with each other. My name is Manipal and now you all can introduce yourself one by one.'

I was happy to get away from books for a while and happier still when we dispersed for the recess.

After the break, we were divided into groups of three on the basis of our roll numbers, before entering the Physics laboratory for conducting our experiments. My group members were Aditya and Kunal. Aditya was somewhat stocky and short in height. Within a few minutes I discovered that he was more studious than any of us. Kunal was of the same height as Aditya but athletically built and livelier in nature. We were assigned the practical for measuring the viscosity of water. I was not at all interested in performing the experiment but Aditya was serious about conducting the experiment. After much ado, I reluctantly agreed to join them in their quest for failure. Although for a major portion of time I sat glued to my stool, watching both of them work their ass out in setting up the instrument. My moral support was always there with them. When, after repeated efforts, they were not able to set up the instrument, I took on the responsibility – not to perform the experiment, but to call the lab assistant.

'Sir, we are not able to perform the experiment,' Aditya said with disappointment writ large on his face. 'Can you please help us?'

'Boys, this instrument is faulty. Why don't you join that group to perform the experiment? They are doing the same practical,' he said, pointing his finger to another group.

I started laughing but stopped midway when I saw Aditya glaring at me. 'Shit man, why didn't he give us that precious piece of information earlier?'

'Because he wanted you to understand that it is of no use to perform the practical. Just chill *yaar*. Why are you taking this so seriously?' I said laughingly.

Reluctantly Aditya and Kunal too joined me on their stools. Soon it was 4:10 p.m. and we were allowed to leave the lab.

I was tired, really tired. I never thought that a college meant studying from morning till evening. I really felt like screwing myself every single second.

But my busy schedule was not over yet because something more was about to happen. I had hardly jumped into the bed out of weariness, when someone knocked on the door with all his might.

Thump, thump! Bang, bang! I resisted opening the door

at first but finally succumbed to the continuous banging and hammering.

'What?' I shouted, opening the door.

A frail boy stood outside the door.

'The seniors are calling everyone to be out in the field,' he announced in a voice that sounded like coming from someone else's mouth. '*Chalo, jaldi karo.* Get ready.'

There was no time to identify the name of the voice. 'Why are they calling?' I asked in a feeble tone.

'I don't know but everyone has to go out. They have sent me to call everyone who is not on the field,' he said in an authoritative tone with pride.

'Where are the other guys?'

'Most of them have already reached the field. Only some like you are left. *Chalo, chalo, jaldi karo* and why are you not following the dress code?'

'That's none of your business,' I said, in an irritated toned, duly irked at his authoritative tone.

'Okay, I am going to call the others. Reach the field immediately.'

'Okay, okay. Go and call the others. I will reach the field on my own,' I said crossly and banged the door shut.

"Oh my God, what should I do? What is gonna happen?" I thought while putting on my uniform.

While going towards the ground, I saw some of the first-year students running towards the field, that too in a line. Soon we were sitting on the lush green grass and listening with our heads down.

It was the voice of a boy from eastern Uttar Pradesh as was obvious from his accent. 'Guys, this is not ragging. You all are here because it is for your own good ("Yeah, who wants to die at 18?" I thought). In this college nobody will help, nobody – neither your faculty nor that bloody warden. Only your seniors will be there to help you in any and all your troubles.' (Sounds amazing, I mean, a lamb having a tiger to serve as his assistant.)

'You need books; we will give them to you. You need tips for survival here and only we can give you those. But the question here is that why should *we* help a bunch of *idiots* like you who don't even know us? Why?' he continued his speech like a local leader offering solace to the flood victims.

'We are having great bonding with our seniors but we won't have that provision for you if you are not gonna cooperate with us.' This was the voice of another boy. 'Respect your seniors and the rest will be taken care of because we can survive without you all, but you can't.'

'One more thing, this is the beginning of the technical phase of your life, so everything here is technical. We are your technical fathers and technical mothers; the third-year students are your technical grandparents and so on. So if someone calls you a mother******, it only refers to your seniors and it's nothing personal. So, now since you all know about our technical relations, just chill, *yaar*.' With this, the first boy ended his speech.

'Now, who plays football?' asked another husky voice.

Some hands were raised and their names duly noted down. Soon players of volleyball and basketball were also gone. Now only a handful was left, including me, seated there.

'Who is Anshul?' someone suddenly asked. I promptly stood up.

'Come here,' ordered a voice.

I started walking in the direction of the voice.

'You daughter******, where are you going? Look up and come here.'

A picture flashed in my mind about my juniors. Hesitantly I looked up and located the possessor of the voice before starting to move towards him.

'Good evening, sir.'

'So you are Afzal's friend?'

'Yes, sir.'

'So he must have told you about this college.'

'Yes, sir.'

'So why the f*** did you come here?'

'I didn't have any other good option.'

'You are looking smart.'

'Thank you sir, but I am not that smart.'

'Don't argue.'

'But, sir, I didn't argue.'

'I said stop arguing,' he snapped.

'But, sir….'

'You are still arguing.'

'Sorry, sir.'

'You need to learn faster.'

I smiled.

'Are you smiling?' he asked

'No, sir,' I instantly wiped that sucking smile from my face.

'You mean I am lying. How dare you say so? Am I blind?' he shouted at the top of his voice.

'No, sir,' I said, cursing the moment I smiled.

'Then what the hell do you mean?' he screamed.

'Sir, I… I…,' I stammered.

'Yes come on, asshole, what the hell did you mean? C'mon, spit it out,' he bellowed like a raging bull.

'Sorry, sir.'

'Mate, you seem to be learning too fast,' he said, giving a crooked smile.

I was amazed at his sudden change of temper.

'I am a friend of Afzal. He told me about you. Do you know me?' he asked.

'No, sir.'

'Oh, wow! I know your name, your branch and everything and you don't know anything about me. Amazing indeed!'

'Sorry, sir.'

'What the hell do you mean by saying sorry?' he thundered.

I remained silent.

'So what would you call Afzal?'

'Sir… sir, I will call him Sir.'

'Are you sure?'

'Yes, sir.'

'Do you smoke?'

'No, sir.'

'Are you sure?'

'Yes, sir.'

'Drink?'

'No, sir.'

'What, no sir? Never ever interrupt me in between.'

'Sorry, sir.'

'If I ever find you smoking and drinking, I promise it won't be good for your health. So tell me right now if you smoke?'

'No sir, I don't smoke.'

'Saw any of that kind of movie?'

'What kind, sir?'

'You moron, I mean that kind of a movie, THAT KIND?'

'Exactly what kind? If you were to only explain, it would be more helpful, sir. I really didn't understand,' I said, hazily getting an idea of the kind of movies he meant.

'Blue film, you idiot. Have you seen any?' he barked.

'No, sir,' I blurted out.

'I told you not to lie in front of me.'

'I am not lying, sir.'

'You are arguing again.'

'Sorry, sir.' It was indeed a difficult situation when you are being convicted for something you have not ever done in your life and that too without giving you the chance to present your justification.

'I am going to give you an assignment...'

'Yes, sir.'

'I told you not to interrupt me in between,' he yelled.

'Sorry, sir,' I apologised.

'Find out the names of your room-fathers and myself within two days.'

'Okay, sir.'

'You can go now.'

'Excuse me, sir. May I know your name please?'

'Don't try to be over-smart because this is not the format for asking the names.'

'Sorry, sir.'

'*GO*,' he barked in exasperation.

'Goodnight, sir,' I left with this parting shot.

* * * * *

'Oye, blue shirt,' a voice called from behind my back the moment I was quietly trying to enter the hostel.

'Yes, sir?'

'Come with me.'

I was petrified and guessed that my end was near. Going in the seniors' lobby meant one had opted for one's own death.

'Hey, where are you going? Don't you know this is the seniors' lobby? Stay right here. I will be back just now.'

At the threshold, the saintly voice of the same senior relieved me of my fears, although temporarily.

I waited like an obedient slave. After a gap of fifteen minutes, he came back with a pile of papers. 'Copy this assignment on these A-4 sheets as soon as possible and take help from two or three more juniors. Okay? Anyways, what is your name, branch and room number?'

'Anshul Verma from Computer Science and Engineering; Room number is 155,' I muttered after mustering all my energy.

'Okay, now go.'

'Goodnight, sir.'

4

The Jail

Back in the hostel, the talk of the town was ragging and to put it in a more suave manner, it was the 'personality development programme'. Some were afraid and vowed not to visit the field any more, while a few of the other guys were excited about the whole bloody practice. It was the latter group who filled us with their experiences on the field by going over them again and again. But soon these stories of personal rendezvous became redundant, to be replaced by new and, most of the times, fake encounters.

Nobody wanted to be left in the race of being the most loved junior among the seniors because it was believed that if you were the most sought after among the second-year students, you were the one to have the last say in hostel matters. But the seniors themselves were divided into many small groups and it was up to the fresher to decide whom to be loyal to.

Anyhow we found every incident enjoyable and we instantly decided to stick together. This was the time when we all were looking for friends and this mutual need and common concern of PDP brought us close in our initial days.

All of a sudden a whole new world lay in front of me. I realised that living in a small suburb had not given me the real taste of life. In the midst of thousands of students, I was forced to go into the nitty-gritty of things in an entirely new fashion. And soon the hostel became a favourite place for many of us, so much so that I rarely felt the need to visit home even during my holidays.

* * * * *

'Hey, stop the goddamn bus,' shouted someone from the seat behind me.

We were returning from the city after a tiring visit to the Bareilly town or was it a village, I cannot tell for the life of me.

'Why? What happened?' Akshay asked, turning back from his seat. I found myself sandwiched between him and another boy.

'There is a girl who is unable to board the bus,' said the boy behind me.

We all turned to look outside. We saw a short and thin girl shouting for the bus to stop.

"That girl is from our college?" I asked myself, but prompt came the reply from the back seat, 'Yeah, you are from CS, aren't you?' he said, while shifting on my seat.

The bus stopped and the issue of the girl took a back seat.

'Yeah? You too?'

'Definitely, man, I am in EC + CS (a class consisted of both EC and CS students for a period of one year as the syllabus was same) and you know what, CS guys rock?'

I didn't fully understand the reason for his over-enthusiasm.

'You are not drunk, right?'

'No man, I don't drink. Why did you ask that?'

'Nothing, I was just asking. I saw some first-year student entering the model wine-shop today,' I tried to divert the topic, which I had accidentally raised.

'Hi, I am Aayush, and you?' and I had succeeded.

'Anshul.'

'Which room?'

'155…and you?'

'160.'

'That means we are on the same floor. Then how come I have never seen you before?'

'I have seen you a couple of times,' he replied. I reddened somewhat.

'So what took you out on this Monday outing?'

'Seniors; I mean, I didn't want to be left alone in the hostel to be bogged down by the seniors, and you?'

'Same here. Do you know where this Butler Plaza is?'

'The same place from where we boarded our bus today.'

'*What*? You are joking, right? Tell me aren't you kidding?'

'No, mate, I am serious. But why are you so disappointed?'

'You mean that small structure with five something showrooms and numerous small shops is Butler Plaza? Oh God, I thought it would be some kind of a mall or something like that,' I said unbelievingly.

'Well I too was disappointed knowing this, but it's okay.' At that time I had felt that disappointment was not the right word but I wasn't able to remember anything grander than that.

'So, what did you do today?'

'Saw a movie.'

'I thought going to a theatre was not allowed. Anyways, what was it like?'

'Disastrous and more than that, the theatre was worse that the film itself. It was really a torture sitting on a seat filled with nails and that too for a movie which made no head or tail."

Aayush laughed and so did I, though my bottom was still paining.

Aayush was a guy of medium height and a bit stocky, but blessed with a handsome physique. He had small eyes, pointed noise, broad shoulders and hailed from Allahabad. He was one of the top rankers in encounters with seniors and the more the encounters, the greater the gossip. We were diametrically opposite, but he was not narrow-minded like many of the other hostellers when it came to talking about girls, girls and more girls. Even though he was from a boys' school, he was broad-minded and that is where we had struck a chord.

* * * * *

The first semester was proceeding at a furious pace. I had never imagined that college could be so boring. Spending eight ridiculous hours every day in the confines of the college was an unimaginable torture.

The first thing that became pretty clear was that the college was running on whims and fancies of its managing director, who believed in bringing back the era of the 18th century when women spent their lives covered behind larger-than-life *pallus* (the end of a sari that is used to cover their head) and when it was a socially accepted rule for a boy and a girl to be nothing else but a brother and sister.

Frustration was the only sentiment that was apparent in the atmosphere. I had read somewhere that bullshit can take you only up to a certain height, but sincerity is not bound by any of these limits. Here, however, all such rules and principles did not seem to exist. Sycophancy was the rule with unqualified, incompetent persons serving as heads of departments, chief warden, Dean, and even principal.

India is a democracy but this declaration never existed within the premises of the Girdhari Lal Smarak College of Engineering & Technology. Every other day, we stared at the notice-board for yet another funky or senseless set of instructions like co-roaming in not allowed, people in groups are not allowed, staying in the hostel during college hours is not allowed, going outside the campus in the evenings is not allowed, canteen is not allowed…not allowed, not allowed and *more not alloweds*.

Nevertheless, people still found reasons to cheer themselves up in spite of the fact that being happy too was not allowed in the campus.

* * * * *

'Stop staring at her,' Vineet said in a terse whisper.

Vineet was an agile-looking, bespectacled, dark guy with a legendary temper which seemed to rest on the tip of his nose, as if waiting to jump out. His slender, athletic build comprising long hands with even longer fingers, with outstandingly jet black hair imparted him a rather uncouth look. He was the epitome of a cynic. He was very talkative with an unusual way of laughing, but he was a man whom one could trust any time of the day with anything.

'What?' Eashaan asked absently.

Eashaan was about 5 feet 9 inces tall, with a more than healthy build. His father was a businessman. His face oozed out the conceit of a rich brat and a black mole just below his right eye made him look like a mischief-monger. His hair was longer than usual and covered almost the whole back side of his neck. He was a true embodiment of a messed-up moneyed guy.

'I said, stop doing that,' Vineet repeated irritatingly.

'Huh?' Eashaan said, gaping at Deepti.

Deepti was almost 5 feet 2 inches with an orange shade as her skin colour. She had a bulky figure with fat hanging loose from her sides. She had large eyes and a prominent lower lip. Her face was filled with orange marks and fine hair. She sat with Saniya, whom she considered her best friend. What is more, no one had ever seen her talk to any boy.

'Are you planning to do something else apart from just staring at her like a moron? Are you going to pay attention to what I am saying or do I leave?' Vineet asked, displaying his foul mood.

'Okay, that's enough,' he said and stood up.

'Hey Vineet, okay, okay, just tell me what were you saying?' Eashaan asked, coming back to his senses.

'Why don't you talk to her instead of ogling at her like a roadside rascal?' asked Vineet, who was at the end of his tethers.

'I don't know…'

'You don't know? What do you mean by you don't know?' asked Vineet, almost shouting.

'I mean I just don't know,' replied Eashaan, trying to calm him down by making him sit down.

'Relax, Vineet.'

'You mean you don't know whether you like her or not?' Vineet continued, without any intention of calming down.

'You know that's not true. She is the only girl I have ever loved.'

'Then why don't you tell her this?'

'It's not that simple as it seems,' said Eashaan, trying to defend himself.

'Yeah, of course, now don't start it all over again,' Vineet said, in a scornful tone.

'Buddy, I am not joking. She is really awesome. I mean she is the most amazing girl in this whole world. I had never believed in love at first sight but now all this is happening to me. I really don't know what to do. Vineet, I won't be able to face her rejection,' Eashaan mumbled in a dreamy voice.

'Okay, if she is so good, then let me propose to her. Then it will be cool. You can gape at her as long as you want and you will also be free from any headache of revealing your feelings,' Vineet said in a terse voice.

'Why, why are you looking at me like this? No, no, I am not going to do anything for you.'

'Man, I think that's a great idea,' said Eashaan with his eyes shining brightly.

'I don't care for any of your great ideas,' Vineet said, looking horrified.

'Please, please, please, please, p...l...e...a...s...e.'

'No, please, nothing.'

'Please.'

'This is the last time I am doing anything for you.'

'Thank you so very much. M...u...a....h...h...h!' Eashaan said, kissing Vineet.

'Crap man, you are so...'

'I know.'

'But you also have to do something.'

'So how are you planning to talk to her? Do you want me to do anything to help you?' asked Eashaan, looking truly excited.

'No thanks a lot, I will do it myself. But don't wander around when we are talking. I will call you when you are needed.'

* * * * *

But the task was not that easy as it seemed initially. Deepti's face was closed like a vault and due to the various layers of creams and lotions plastered on, it was more than difficult to judge whether she approved of Eashaan's eyes on her body all the time or not. Vineet decided to gauge the temperature of the waters by trying to befriend Deepti. However, this was easier said than done because Vineet's temper didn't encourage the sweet talk that is a favourite among girls. And that's why every time he went to talk to Deepti, he invariably returned in the foulest of moods, cursing everyone including the girls, and Eashaan especially.

Love was indeed in the air.

5

My First Mistake

Often in the quiet of my room, I wondered why I had met her, but sometimes answers are not enough to explain everything.

She was around 5 feet 2 inches tall, fair-complexioned with sharp features and an unusually long nose. She talked with an unorthodox accent. Going by her looks, she was the girl any boy would have dreamt of dating, but even I hadn't realised it for long. She certainly seemed to be the dream girl of many. We met during a blood donation camp that was organised in the first week of October by the college authorities. As I told you, my college had never let any opportunity go by to suck our blood. We all were sitting in a narrow passageway in the hospital with Akshay sitting next to me. I was feeling a bit nervous surrounded by seniors, among whom, most were from the second year.

After donating our precious blood, Akshay and I decided to spend the rest of our time away from the confines of the hospital. We chose to take a round of the rest of the hospital from outside. But soon the fear of seniors drew us inside the bus, forcing us to return. We were discussing the college, with him doing all the talking and I acting like a good listener. Soon Avantika, my source of admiration and another girl named Tina, came and sat down on the seat next to ours.

Tina was a Punjabi, shorter and stockier than Avantika but fairer than her; in fact, her skin colour was white. She was blessed with a long, pointed nose and a long plait hung loose on her back.

'Hi, this is Tina and I am Avantika,' Avantika said to us.

'Hello, I am Akshay and this is Anshul,' Akshay replied with a broad smile enveloping his face. No doubt the company of the girls had cast its magical impact on his spirits.

'So, what were you guys talking about – college or something else?'

'Yeah, sort of.'

Tina and I merely stood like silent bystanders while Akshay and Avantika participated in the dialogue.

'So, how do you like our city?'

'It's nice,' Akshay said promptly. Looking at the effort he was putting in, I couldn't stop from smiling which Tina noticed immediately.

'What is so funny? Why are you smiling?' she asked in a bit of a husky voice.

'Nothing, I was just thinking about the city.'

'What? I don't understand?' Avantika said.

'Well, last Monday, I made the mistake of going to the city and now I have decided that under normal circumstances, I won't do it again.'

'Why? Did anything go wrong?' Avantika looked confused and so did Tina.

'Well, nothing went wrong but nothing went right. I won't say that there is not even a single mall in the city because that would be a thing beyond expectation for the next ten years, but surely there could be a good theatre somewhere around! There are many more things which I don't want to discuss in detail but what surprises me is how people can call this a city!' I complained.

'Yeah, that I agree but still it is a peaceful city,' Tina retorted.

'Hey, why are we discussing all this? C'mon, let's tell each other something about ourselves,' Akshay interrupted as he wanted to be the focus of attention.

'Okay, okay, me first,' Avantika said with a child-like eagerness.

'As you please, ma'am,' Akshay said with a broad smile.

'I am Avantika and I hail from Bareilly itself. I had done my schooling at St. Anthony's and what about you?' she said, while looking at me.

'I am Anshul and I had done my schooling from Delhi Public School.'

'But DPS is a co-ed, isn't it?'

'Yeah, it is, but why are you asking this?'

'Nothing, it's just that you don't seem to belong to a co-ed school. You are so shy; aren't you?' Avantika asked, smiling.

'Really, you think so?' I asked sarcastically with a smile on my face.

'Yes, I do think so.'

'Well, then you are seriously wrong. I do have many friends and many of them are girls.'

'But, your female friends, whoever they are, won't be

more attractive than me,' she said with a mischievous smile dancing on her lips.

'Well, I think you have some misconception about your looks. Certainly they are prettier than any of the girls of our college,' I said, recovering from the shock her comment had caused.

'You are saying this only because they are your friends,' she said with the same smile playing around her lips.

"Think as you please,' I said, wondering why the hell I was discussing this.

That was our first meeting. Although we were in the same class, I hadn't been aware of her existence prior to this meeting.

* * * * *

Tina's birthday was approaching near and we remembered that she had invited us to her house. I agreed hesitantly but I was not sure whether I wanted to visit her or not.

'Who else is coming?' I asked Tina.

'Well, Ravi is coming with Avantika and Kruti and there are school friends. Anyways, why are you asking this? You are coming, *naa*?'

'Yeah, I am coming, but I was thinking…'

'Don't think anything. In any case, you didn't wish me on my b'day,' Avantika said, joining us.

'Your birthday? When was that?'

'It was in August, just three days after the college opened,' she said scornfully.

'O…h…well, ma'am, as a matter of fact, at that time we hardly knew each other, so there was no question of wishing you on your birthday,' I said smilingly.

'Now you have the chance to rectify your mistake. So I hope you are coming, right?' she asked tantalisingly.

'Okay, okay, I am coming.'

'It's on Monday, 12 o'clock,' Tina interrupted.

'Monday, 12 o'clock it is.'

* * * * *

The ragging was continuing at a ferocious pace despite our hoping for the torture to cease with the fresher's party. Due to the bloody administration's interference, it had been extended till the end of the first semester as the seniors had complained about the lack of opportunities to fuck us.

'Fuck this management and fuck our seniors,' we cursed them wholeheartedly.

* * * * *

When we reached Tina's house, Ravi was already there, talking to Kruti and Tina. Kruti too was our classmate but neither Akshay nor I had ever talked to her till that day. I was feeling rather uneasy seated in the midst of them and listening to their girlish conversation. Most of the males were those with whom I had never ever dreamed of interacting and never would have done so, had this get-together not happened. So I excused myself from their company and went outside.

'Why have you come outside?' a voice from behind startled me.

It was Avantika with Mandakini. Mandakini was her friend from college. She was from a rich Punjabi family and true to her genes, she was overly healthy, fair in complexion and a formidable front. Her world revolved around the novels she carried with her, possibly to counter her loneliness.

'Nothing, I was just getting bored inside my room. What about you?'

'You were telling me about your friends that day, in the bus.'

'Yeah, what about them?' I asked.

'Nothing, where are they? I mean, what are they doing?' she answered, looking flustered at the question.

"Some of them are doing B.Tech just like us, while a few have joined the NDA and some others are pursuing their B.Sc., etc. What about yours?' I asked.

'What about your girlfriends?' she fired the next shot in return.

'Why are you interested in them? Why are you asking this?'

'Ummm…nothing,' she stammered.

'You are still single, aren't you?' I asked in a teasing manner.

'What else do you think?' she flushed.

'Because it is on your face,' I said, grinning. Mandakini too joined us now. 'I think Tina might want us inside,' I added.

'Yeah, let's go inside,' Mandakini said.

Tina was looking pretty and refreshingly different, may be because she was not in her college outfit. After lunch, somebody suggested that we play Truth and Dare. I don't generally find such games entertaining, but when you are in the midst of a pack of the fair sex, your opinion really doesn't count much. Soon after starting the game, I found myself facing an innocent question: "Who is your crush in CS branch?"

The question was easy, but the answer was tough because

till that time I had never thought about any girl of CS in that sense. 'I don't have any,' I said it as a plain fact.

'You can't fool us into believing you,' Avantika said.

'No really, there isn't any actually.'

'You had chosen TRUTH, so tell us the truth,' Avantika continued unrelentingly.

'Well, I am telling the truth.' But no one wanted to hear such a boring answer.

'Are you scared, or is she present here?'

I remained silent because I thought it best to keep mum, but it proved a big mistake because Avantika judged my silence as a 'yes'. What is more, all of them felt the same and pounced on me with more force.

'I have an idea. Why don't you give that teddy to the one you like, as we all know that she is one of us,' Ravi suggested, pointing at a soft toy.

What an idiotic idea it was, but none of them seemed to believe me.

'Yeah, that's a great idea,' Avantika said and handed the teddy to me.

I cursed myself for choosing TRUTH rather than DARE. Now I had to think something very fast and quick. After a long silence I said, 'Okay, Tina this teddy is for you because today is your b'day and you are looking very pretty.'

I presented her the teddy and somehow managed to get over the delicate question.

'But this is not the answer,' Avantika retorted.

'Well, this is the only answer I have right now. Come on, let's continue with the game.'

The game continued for some more time but Avantika's

mischievous look told me that though the party was over, the danger was not over yet.

* * * * *

Next day, in college I was trying to complete some pending work in my free lecture time when Tina came and sat down beside me. Soon Avantika followed and sat down on the bench in front of me. My sixth sense instantly told me that something was amiss and before I could figure out what the matter was, Tina started to babble about her b'day party.

'You don't consider us your friends,' Tina said.

'Yeah, she is right,' Avantika joined her in her tirade.

'Otherwise you would have told us the truth yesterday,' Tina continued.

'You would have told us whom you liked if you had looked upon us as your friends,' Avantika taunted.

I was dumbfounded by their sudden attack but tried to remain calm and silent. 'I told you the answer yesterday itself,' I said after a pause.

'As a matter of fact, we don't think that was the truth,' Avantika said, rolling her eyes.

'Well, as a matter of fact, I think it's the contrary,' I said in the same tone. 'So, what gifts did you get yesterday?'

'Don't change the topic,' Avantika said pointedly.

'Keep that small finger down since the topic has already changed,' I said, grinning at her. 'So, Tina you were telling me about your presents.'

Tina looked at Avantika and then at me with a weak smile. I controlled myself from smiling, while looking at their faces.

* * * * *

I was in the Physics lab when Tina came to me and blurted out, 'I know whom you like.'

I smiled and said, 'Tina it's nothing, believe me.'

'You don't worry, I won't tell her about it.'

'Whom would you not tell? Who is she?'

I said nothing after hearing the name but a smile came on my face. Many a times I have wondered at myself as to why the hell did I smile so much! And the simple answer that seemed apparent was that I was a born idiot.

'I won't talk to you ever. How could you do this to me? How could you?'

My private moments were shattered by the sudden rebuke from Avantika. 'What? I mean, what happened? What did I do?' I wondered while knowing precisely what was it all about.

'You always considered Tina a better friend of yours, didn't you? I should have known.'

'Why...why do you think so?' I faltered again.

Our conversation was definitely not going the way I wanted it.

'You had told Tina about her, but not me. That is why,' she grumbled now a tad louder.

'But I didn't tell her anything. Who told you?' The situation was getting out of hand.

But she marched right away from there as if I had said something very vicious.

* * * * *

Life provides you with mental respite whenever you need your head the most. That evening I thought about all the good things the boys would have said about Avantika and even about my prospects for a future with her as my girlfriend. It looked dimly bright. Although I was yet not sure whether I liked her or not, only God knew why the hell I decided to tell her whom I vaguely liked?

It was recess when I called her the next day.

'Hey, how are you?'

'I am fine,' she said plainly.

'You were asking yesterday about the girl on whom I have a crush. Do you still want to know?'

She remained silent.

'Sorry, I didn't get your answer,' I persisted.

'I don't want to know.'

'Okay, as you wish, but I want to tell you that you are the girl on whom I have a crush.'

She stared at me with surprise and went outside. I stood rooted to the spot, watching her disappear through the doors.

The damage had been done and when I entered the class after recess, everything had changed.

6

I was Crushed

After recess, Tina approached me and said in a tone of anger mixed with worry, 'You shouldn't have done that.'

Damn these girls! First they harass you till your deathbed and when you tell them something, they blame you for saying anything.

'Where is Avantika?' I was getting worried now. *Welcome to the real world, mate,* I thought.

'Canteen,' she gave a curt reply.

'What did she say?'

'Well, she didn't expect anything like this. So she was shocked and somewhat angry.'

Now, what did she mean by 'angry'? I only told her that she was my crush for the time being and I think it was normal. Well, everyone had a crush or two in one's life. Isn't it?

'I want to talk to her.'

'No, just wait for some more time. She needs time.'

I really liked that sentence because I too needed some time. 'Okay, I'll wait.'

* * * * *

Two days elapsed. I thought now it was time to do some talking, instead of thinking. So I reached the class early in the morning. It was deserted. She entered soon with a bunch of other day-scholars.

'I want to talk to you,' I cornered her.

'Okay,' said she. Did I see a smile on her face? No, it was a normal expression of hers. I walked out of the classroom and she followed.

'Okay, what is it?' she asked, without looking at me.

'Look, Avantika, whatever happened that day…I mean, I didn't want to hurt you or anything like that.'

'I understand.'

'Apart from what I said that day, I still want our friendship more than anything else. I think it's natural for you to like someone just as you dislike someone.' The only thing that was bothering me during the whole tête-à-tête was her perpetual glance sideways, instead of looking directly at me. A moment ago I had been anxious to talk to her but now all I wanted was to end this discussion soon.

'Look Anshul, I think it is too early for me to say anything, but still I want to say that we are friends and will remain so. I just…just don't want to ruin our friendship.'

'Avantika, we are friends and will remain like that.'

She smiled and finally looked at me, but not for long. The first lecture was about to start and we hurried back to the class.

* * * * *

Some things are easier said than done. In no time I knew that we couldn't just be friends only, no matter how hard we tried. It was bound to be on our mind and it couldn't be a simple friendship. I could sense her nervousness whenever we talked, though we talked rarely and most of the time it was in the company of Tina. Also I couldn't help but be self-conscious whenever she was around. Something definitely was not right between us.

And one day, I went to talk to her. But she said, 'Anshul, I don't want to talk to you any more.'

I was astounded, but somehow managed to say, 'Okay.'

* * * * *

We didn't talk for a few days. Then one day, when the class was almost empty, I confronted her, 'Avantika, what's the matter?'

'It's nothing.'

'What do mean by nothing? You are not talking to me without a reason; I want to know the reason,' I said in a stern voice.

Reluctantly she said, 'I have heard that you've been telling everyone in the hostel that I have accepted your proposal and we are somewhat like a couple.'

'What are you talking about? Who said that to you?' I asked in a bewildered tone.

'I can't tell you who it is, but I know it's true,' she said emphatically.

'So, if you trust that somebody's words more than mine, then we should definitely not talk,' I said, somehow controlling my anger as I walked away.

* * * * *

Friends are the best teachers in one's life because they teach you lessons after you've hurt yourself badly. I was really very angry, not with her but myself and at the same time I was somewhat happy for myself; very happy.

That night, while remembering our last friendly meet in college, I felt myself smiling even though I tried hard to feel sad. I was angry but couldn't help smiling.

It was no longer a secret that we were not on talking terms and obviously everyone knew about it and most were pleasantly surprised! Tina knew about these things much more clearly than anyone else, but she was still a friend. The quality I liked in her was that she behaved more maturely than Avantika (or so at that time). She was a friend of Avantika, but she never asked awkward questions about her and neither did I ever mention Avantika in front of her. It was better to leave things as they were instead of carrying on with a post mortem.

* * * * *

We were entering the month of November when suddenly someone whispered in our ears, "WHOA, EXAMS ARE COMING!"

The first semester exams were approaching near and in between there was to be a mid-semester exam based on the pattern of the end semester and which was very crucial for our internal assessment. All of a sudden we found ourselves caught in the hectic examination schedule and a lot of study material to cram in no time. The mother of all the tensions was round the corner.

Everything grew quiet. The hostel, where every other day seemed like an *Eid* or *Diwali*, now appeared like a cemetery to me. I began to get edgy at the drop of a hat and everyone seemed to behave like me. It was winter and being close to Nainital, the place had its own shortcomings, which now became apparent. While it was chilly outside, the empty lobbies appeared icier as the tension started building minute by minute. Every senior batch in the past had been witness to some high performers. In order to continue the tradition, everyone in our batch was vying to be like them. We all were busy cramming our bulky books and the basic necessities like eating, sleeping and ogling at girls had taken a back seat. I was never considered one of the top-rate horses. For the faculty, I was like a non-existent glitch and my classmates knew me more as a guy who got dumped in the first semester itself as I knew nothing about Engineering Drawing and SOM.

The mid-semester exams started and for the following five days we were cut off from the outside world. The days appeared short and the books like a never-ending travail. At last the exams got over and finally our real test of B. Tech education arrived with all its force. The first examination was in Maths, the weakest link in my fourteen years of education. I was sitting on the bed, half reclining and staring at the book with the hope that it would unveil some magical strategies for solving those puzzling questions that were to come next day. Time flew like a jet plane and I kept on sweating like a pig with every passing second. I tried to take forty winks but it was of no use. I slept only for four hours and even that was filled with the wildest of dreams. I felt as though my head had become an airbus that was about to crash. *I must take a bath*, I thought.

Our centre was at a distance of 15 kms, so we left the campus at 7:30 in the morning as the exams were scheduled for 9:30 a.m. Everyone was engrossed in his or her notes when seated in the bus. I also tried to test my vigour but God knows when I went to sleep, lolling my head from one side to the other. All of a sudden the bus stopped with a rude jolt and I woke up with a start. Oh my God, how come we had reached so early? It was only 9:00 a.m.!

"Omigawd, omigawd, I am dead. I am screwed. Oh gawd what should I do?"

"Calm down, calm down Anshul and just relax," I tried to console myself. "Just take some deep breaths."

'Are you okay?' Aayush asked.

'Yeah, I am not okay,' I replied feebly.

'Relax buddy, this is just another exam,' he said.

'I know, but I think I am forgetting everything. What was the formula for Fourier transformation?'

'Fourier transformation? Oh that's easy. It was…gosh, I forgot where the book is.'

'It's here,' I said, showing him the formula.

'Okay, I think we should go inside, otherwise there will be no end to it,' Aayush suggested.

'Okay,' I said.

I was sitting in the examination hall with my eyes closed and mind blank. Suddenly a thought flashed through my mind and it was AVANTIKA! C'mon man, what was I doing? I opened my eyes and saw the paper lying in front of me. I scanned it with my eyes expanded twice their original size. It was easy. I felt a wave of confidence surge though my chest. After all, it was just another paper.

The next paper was on Mechanics and we got only one day for its preparation. The course seemed as vast as an ocean with no beginning or end. I had been studying non-stop for the last eleven hours but I saw no hopes of completing my revision on time.

When I sat for the exams, I was completely exhausted at the sixeen hours of continuous mental workout. I had hardly slept the previous night and I think none in CS had. After looking at the question paper, I thanked God that my hard work hadn't gone in vain. On leaving the examination hall, I felt I had conquered the world and so had everyone.

After the Mechanics exam, the rest of the exams seemed like a walkover. Exams were over and now the formality of appearing in the practical tests remained. In the viva, we were generally called in groups of four. Aditya was the first in our group, followed by Kunal, myself and Kruti. So the first question was faced by Aditya which was then passed on to us. I tried to concentrate on the answers given by Aditya and Kunal before presenting my answer which was an amalgamation of their answers.

Everyone had been looking forward to the semester break with the exception of me because in our college, we hardly got holidays. As soon as the practical exams ended, we left for our respective homes. For me even a 10-day break was a long time to be at home, but I had no other alternative.

Before that, a big challenge awaited us at the platform. The seniors were also leaving with us and most of them were in the same train as us. They had not got enough opportunities to torture us so far. Now I knew why it was comfortable to remain in the safe confines of the hostel than in the vulnerable bogey of the train.

7

My Second Mistake

It was forbidden to wear jeans, belt and wrist-watch for any junior but in the excitement of going home, I had broken the dress code happily.

Aayush and I reached the station well on time. He had a reserved seat, while I was travelling in the general compartment. There were still twenty minutes left for the train to move, so I decided to wander around on the platform. As luck would have it, I ran straight into one whom I wouldn't have wanted to meet in my wildest of dreams.

One of our notorious seniors spotted me and called me over. I went and stood in front of him, looking at my third button once again and praying to God for mercy. At the same time I was cursing myself for not following the dress code. He said nothing for some time, so I lifted my head to look at his face. A saint-like smile played on his face. I felt relieved and tried to smile, but as soon as my lips stretched themselves a bit, his expression underwent a marked change and my smile froze where it was. I looked sideways for help but there was no one closeby to come to my rescue.

'Hello Anshul,' he said with a devious smile.

'Good afternoon, sir,' I hiccupped.

'How are you?'

'I was…I mean I am fine, sir, thank you," I stammered.

'Is that a pair of jeans?'

'Yes…sir.'

'Oh my God, a pair of jeans? Gosh, I have never seen jeans before. Can I touch it?'

'Sorry, sir.'

'I said can I touch it? You know it was my childhood dream to wear jeans some day. Please, please let me touch it,' he said childishly.

I knew he was teasing me but I couldn't do anything except to obey him.

'Oh my God, I can't believe my eyes. Is that a wrist-watch? A real working one, and is that a belt? Oh yeah, it is a belt. Man, one thing for sure, you are looking great in these gadgets. Why don't you come with me and show this stuff to your other seniors? They will be more than happy to see these things,' he suggested sweetly as if sugar would have melt in his mouth.

'Sir, I am sorry, it won't happen again,' I pleaded.

'Start walking,' he thundered. 'Who are your room-fathers?'

'Sir…respected Eashaan sir, respected…'

'Who?'

'Respected Eashaan sir, SIR,' I said, emphasising more on the last word. 'I remembered it since one of my classmate had the same name.'

'You know him?'

I could sense a ray of hope in that question but my problem was that I had only a vague idea about his having a mole on his face. 'Yes sir, I know him.'

'Okay,' he took me outside the compartment and said, 'Tell me where is he?'

The place was filled with all kind of dogs, I mean, seniors and suddenly my gaze fell on a guy seated inside the bogey, talking to two ordinary looking girls. His face had the same kind of mole I was searching for, though I was far from sure. 'Sir, he is the one,' I took a chance.

'Then call him.'

'EASHAAN sir,' I shouted like a drowning man looking for the last straw to clutch.

Everyone turned to look at me as if I had landed from another planet.

'What happened? Why are you calling me?' the guy with the mole turned towards me.

'He told me to do that,' I pointed at the butcher.

'He said that you are his room-father,' said my tormentor.

'Which room?'

'Sir, Room No. 155,' I replied in a humble but confident tone.

'So, you are Anshul?' On hearing this, my tormentor left me for greener pastures, but not before reminding Eashaan sir about my jeans and belt.

'Yes sir,' I felt relieved as though some heavy weight had been lifted off my chest.

'How did you recognise me?'

'Sir, my roommate told me that you had visited the room but at that time I was not there. He had told me how you looked, so I knew who you were,' I said, trying to sound confident but failing miserably.

'Well, that was a long time ago. You have a good memory, I must say.'

Saale, yaha toh naani yaad aa gayi, toh intna yaad nahi aa sakta, I thought. 'Yes sir, my good luck,' I said.

'Tell me what do you want to have?'

'No sir, it's okay.' It was getting tougher as seconds slipped by.

'No it's not okay. You have to take something.'

'Okay sir, as you please,' I said, thinking I couldn't ask for anything more than this. He reminded me about my stupidity to forget about the dress code which I readily accepted, but as he left, he advised me to enter my compartment without any delay.

The train blew the whistle and started to roll on its wheels. I kept looking outside the window, glad that the experience had not been so fearsome.

* * * * *

Ten days of holiday flew past and soon I found myself breathing again inside my hostel room. Though I had been reluctant to go home for the vacations, now I was no less reluctant to return back to college.

Even though the situation was different and I had become familiar with my batchmates, among them I had very few whom I could call friends. One of them was Shyam, whom I had met on the basketball field at the time of ragging. The introduction was unusual as he had come to me to ask whether I was Anshul. Later, when I asked him how he knew me, his answer took me completely by surprise. He said that I belonged to the same caste as him and that was the reason for his approaching me. He then gave me a lecture on why it was important for us to stay together because if we didn't, then the others could take advantage of us. I found it rather strange because I was not interested in that kind of a social order.

It was then that I understood why the world is so much different than how it is projected in our textbooks. I found that theory took a back seat and realism reigned supreme. He was undeniably a very good orator and his accent made his schooling shine through his pronunciation. He wore spectacles, had a small forehead and thick hair; he was somewhat stocky that reduced his height and made him appear average looking from every angle. However, confidence oozed out from every pore of his body.

Though no one likes to be browbeaten by somebody in one's life, I was fascinated by his ideology. We kept on talking, sitting on the court.

His room was a floor above mine and one of his roommates was called Ved, who was one of the most diplomatic persons I had met and could ever hope to meet. Shyam referred to him as his alter ego but I had my reservations on that. Actually it was I who used to visit Shyam in his room for the simple reason that I didn't like others coming and sitting on my bed and lecture me on what was right or what was wrong. I was however, pretty okay when sitting in someone else's room.

Shyam was very vocal about his X-effect on girls and tended to show off by dropping names of his female friends. His stories generally concluded by depicting the girl crying her heart out on his shoulder or holding his hand. And true to his words, he had befriended Avantika and Mandakini. Unlike Avantika, the latter was an introvert. Since the faculty knew Avantika as she was the only figure among the ciphers, they automatically came to know Mandakini too.

Soon the three of them became very good friends and being in the same group in the lab, helped their cause. The bond was visible at every hour and every place and Shyam loved narrating all that would pass between them. Whenever I asked him why he did not confide about these things to his brother-like friend Ved, his reply invariably was that he did not belong to the same caste as him and so he could not rely on him fully. In reality, he was afraid that if Ved got to know the details of his friendship with Avantika and Mandakini, he could use the friendship to his own advantage.

Shyam used to talk loudly on his mobile despite knowing that they were not allowed to use the instrument in the college. This was so, especially when his so-called female friends made a call to him. One day, while sitting in my room, he took out his cell phone and asked me, 'Do you know whose number this is?'

'I have absolutely no idea, mate,' I said studying J.B. Sharma's book on Electrical Engineering.

'This is the number which every boy would love to know,' he proudly announced.

'Is it 36-24-36?' I said, looking intently at my book.

'Stop reading that goddamn book and just look at this. This number belongs to Avantika; she gave it only to me,' he said with pride.

I looked at him and then at the piece of paper he was holding. Now I understood why he was showing it to me. 'Good for you, but why are you showing it to me?' I asked smilingly before turning back to my book.

'You know her number, don't you?' he asked hesitantly, looking at my smile.

'No, you are the first person to get it,' I said in the same tone.

'No, I was merely asking you,' Shyam said awkwardly.

'I know and it's okay. What will I do with numbers? I don't have any cell phone,' I said matter of factly.

'So you don't have Tina's number?' he asked surprisingly.

'You got it right again.'

'Listen, I have to go to the library,' Shyam said all of a sudden.

'Okay, bye,' I shot back nonchalantly.

From that day onwards his favourite timepass became explaining to me how important he was in the lives of both Avantika and Mandakini and how they didn't do anything without his consent. At times I would get so bored at his boasting that I had to rush to my room to seek refuge.

There are no free lunches in this world and this reality hit me when Shyam, in lieu of his tales about Mandakini and Avantika, asked me to tell him what was transpiring between Tina and me. Though all knew that Tina and I had become good friends but according to Shyam, there could never be a platonic relationship between a boy and a girl.

Soon he started taking liberties with me and began to advise me on matters relating to Tina. This proved to be the last straw for me. I also realised that at times, on the pretext of his friendship with me, he often extracted details from me over trivial matters pertaining to Tina and me. It was much later that I realised that I had revealed more than was necessary and wasted a lot of my time in explaining things to him to get out of sticky situations.

This was the second mistake that I had committed.

8

The Mirage

The growing intimacy between Shyam and Avantika began to bother one other person too. Shubh was a tad shorter in height than any of us. He had a frail body with a sallow complexion and a long pointed nose below his scalp which shone bright due to his sticky hair. He possessed a highly pitched accent in complete contrast to his delicate stature. He was a man of public relations and was known as "Mr Social" in the hostel. He knew everyone and anyone of the college.

Shubh liked Avantika from the core of his heart but was unable to overcome his fear of talking to her. Whenever he drew near her, the loud pounding of his heart against his skeleton could be heard even from the adjacent room. But, unfortunately, Avantika didn't have a clue about Shubh's existence. Shubh spent most of his daytime in college looking intently at Avantika from the last bench and his evenings in sharing his feelings with Vineet.

* * * * *

'Today she was looking very cute,' Shubh said, when lying on his bed and staring at the corner of the roof where the three walls met and vanished into each other.

'Hm…m…m…m,' Vineet nodded his head, looking at Shubh's face.

'She has the most serene-looking face on this whole planet. When I look at her, I just want everything to stop where I it is and keep looking at her as she sits on the second row and not think of anything else.'

'Hm…m…m…m.'

'Every time I see her smile, I start wishing that all my wishes and dreams could come true. But I hate it when that son of a bitch, Shyam, talks to her in the lab, shares her smiles or touches her hand. Today when he was holding her hand in the lab, I felt a strong urge to shoot him right then and there. Vineet, I can't share her with anyone, not even with her parents,' Shubh said, closing his eyes.

'Shubh *yaar*, please stop crying,' pleaded Vineet, abruptly coming to his senses.

'I am not crying *yaar*. These tears are my destiny, I know,' said Shubh, covering his face with his hands.

Vineet just sat there, thinking about Avantika and Deepti.

* * * * *

But the love stories were far from over yet and the magic of love in the air could not spare even Aayush, who held a soft corner for Aarti. She was a bubbly and charming girl but neither very fair nor tall in height. Altogether she had an air that was pleasing. Aayush was somewhat in the same situation as Shubh. Rajiv, who was tall and hefty, was a relative of

Aarti's family friends and his intimacy with Aarti troubled Aayush a lot.

'What are you doing here? Is this a free period?' Aayush shot a question at me on finding me sitting alone.

'Huh? Barkha ma'am is absent, so I was thinking of going back to the hostel.'

'Oh crap! That means I won't be able to see her lovely face today,' Aayush said, rubbing his forehead in distress.

'Why? Which lecture was she supposed to give today in your class?' I asked.

'It was after the recess *yaar*, but never mind. Hey, this is Aarti and Aarti, this is Anshul Verma.'

'Hi Aarti! Vow!'

'What happened?'Aarti asked in surprise.

'Nothing as such; just that I had noticed you once and never realised that you were so stupidly small.'

'I didn't understand,' Aarti said, somewhat offended.

'I mean your height can give a complex to most of the kids.'

'Thanks, that was what I had been waiting to hear since long. Hey, why are you going to the hostel? Come with us and in any case, it is a free period for you too,' Aarti insisted.

I felt thrilled as this was what I had longed for since long; yes, home-cooked food.

'Thanks Aarti, it's been a long time since I ate something good like a home-cooked meal and…' I looked at Aayush to continue, 'you know, what I think – today is not the right time because right now I am feeling very sleepy. So may be some other time would be better. Anyways, thanks for the offer.'

'But…'

'Don't compel him Aarti, it is okay. He can join us some other time though it would have been ideal if he had come,' Aayush interrupted.

Yeah, yeah, as if I don't know how good it would have been, I thought.

'Aayush is absolutely right. Anyways, I have to go. See you then,' I said and left.

* * * * *

Most of my time was spent in Aayush's room with the remaining being spent with Shyam. So, when one day Shyam knocked at my door at one o'clock at night, I knew something was amiss. Since I had restricted my visits to his room, I felt there was too much inside him that was waiting to be spilt out. I reluctantly closed the magazine I was reading as I knew that he would be in my room for at least three hours, if not more. And as expected, he started the conversation in a secretive tone.

'I think Mandakini likes me,' Shyam said.

'What?' I was impressively shocked. 'I mean how can you say such a *ridiculous* thing? Is this a joke or something? I thought you liked Avantika.'

'Yeah, I know it's strange, but Avantika and I are just friends and I know Mandakini likes me.'

I had not idea that things could happen so fast that I would be left behind. 'You think that or do you know that she likes you?' I asked, looking shocked.

'I think she likes me a lot,' Shyam replied confidently.

'And why do you think so? Did she say something to you?' I asked.

'Are you dumb or what? A girl never says such things.'

‘So how do you know this?’ I said in a relaxed tone once I sensed that it was another trick being played by my beloved pal. ‘If she didn’t say anything, how can you say such a thing?’

‘Idiot, everything is not said through words; some things have to be understood,’ he said as a proud owner of this rare quality.

‘You know what? I think you are joking. She is not that kind of a girl,’ I said teasingly. ‘Now, let me concentrate on this article.’

‘So, you don’t believe me?’ he said in an agitated tone.

‘For now, the answer is no.’

‘Okay.’

I was still gazing at the magazine, but through the corner of my eye I could sense his restlessness.

‘I thought you would believe me because you are my friend. That’s why I came to you,’ he said in a hurt voice.

‘I believe you, but still I can’t imagine that the girl you are talking about is Mandakini. Okay, I believe you but stop giving me that look. Alright?’ I tried to end the debate over my loyalty to him.

‘Promise me that you won’t tell anyone abut the things I am going to reveal.’

‘Okay, I promise,’ I said in a sombre tone.

‘At the fresher’s party she was staring at me and I caught her looking at me many times.’

‘Well, that means you were also staring at her,’ I grinned.

‘Stop joking *yaar*. I have also noticed that whenever I talk to Avantika, she keeps staring at us. In the lab also, she always completes my file or makes the diagrams without my asking for it.’

'That's it. I mean I don't think these are sufficient reasons to reach any conclusion. She might just consider you as her friend,' I suggested.

'What are you talking about? What did you do in Avantika's case? And there are other things also which I can't explain.'

Now this was like hitting me below the belt. 'I think you are right. She might be liking you, but the question is whether you like her or not,' I said after a pause, longing for the conversation to come to an end.

'Well, to pass the time in college, she is not bad, but I would not like to have a lifelong affair with her,' he said, showing his teeth.

'Man, then you have got it right. She is perfect for you and I know, sooner or later she will admit her feelings for you,' I said, pretending to be thrilled.

'Are you sure?' he asked excitedly.

Some people just don't want to face daylight. 'Yeah I am sure. Well it's already 2:30 p.m., so let's go to sleep.'

'Okay, goodnight,' he said and left.

I closed the door and heaved a sigh of relief. But the ghost of Mandakini didn't let go of Shyam, who in turn started harassing me with his whacky interpretations about her. One day, as I lay in my bed with my eyes closed after a tiresome day, someone slammed the door.

'Open the door, Anshul,' said a familiar voice from behind the door.

'Who is it? I am sleeping,' I said in a lazy tone.

'Open the door, *yaar*. This is me....Shyam.'

Oh God please, not again, I thought.

The knocking on the door grew louder and at last I got

up, cursing him loudly before opening the door wide. But this time there was more for me than I expected.

'What?' I shouted, but within a second I controlled myself. 'What is she doing here in the boy's hostel?' I was really amazed at what I saw.

'She has left her home and now she is going to live here,' Shyam said.

'Here? What are you saying?' I asked with my eyes wide open with disbelief.

'Here, in your room and what I am saying is true,' Shyam said in a determined voice.

'Have you gone mad or something? And why is she not saying anything? Mandakini, what the fuck is this?' I asked, looking angrily at her.

'Anshul, you are my only hope. If you don't help us, then we are going to commit suicide right here in your room with this poison,' Shyam said, taking out a small bottle from his pocket.

My head began to spin and I had difficulty in standing on my feet.

'So, what do you say?' Shyam asked.

'Shyam, Mandakini, try to understand. Mandakini, why don't you say something?' I asked desperately, trying hard to regain contol over my senses.

'Anshul, so you are not going to help us? Okay, we will die here, right here in front of you and only you will be held responsible for our death,' Shyam said, opening the bottle.

'Look Shyam, just don't do that. We can talk about it calmly and peacefully.'

But he was not prepared to listen to me. I found myself shouting and grabbing his hand to stop him.

'Anshul, open the door,' someone shouted from outside.

I lay flat on my back, breathing hard as though I had been running very fast. I awoke from this horribly vivid dream, clearly able to recall each and everything of what I had seen. It all seemed so real. Someone was still banging at the door with all his might. I tried to get up, but my feet gave way and I could not muster the strength to get up.

'Wait...wait a second,' I cried, with whatever energy I could gather.

Finally I stood up and opened the door to find Aayush sanding in front of me.

'What took you so long? You are still sleeping? See the time; it's 8:15. C'mon, get up for dinner,' Aayush said in a single breath.

I looked at the clock; he was right. 'Okay,' I said.

'What happened to you? You are looking very pale. Is everything alright?' Aayush asked, looking at my face.

'Yeah, yeah, I am alright; just feeling a bit light-headed. Let's go,' I tried to sound normal though deep down I was still living in my dream. Time had come to do something about this because if the dream occurred again, I would definitely go insane.

After dinner, Aayush and I went for a walk.

'What's the matter? You are looking worried,' I said, sensing tension on Aayush's face.

'Nothing *yaar*, it's about Aarti,' Aayush replied.

'What about her?'

'Today she asked me about my past affairs.'

'So, what did you say?'

'Well, I told her about Priya,' he said in a gloomy tone.

'You mean you told her everything? And what did she say?'

I asked in a tone of surprise.

Priya was the girl whom Aayush had liked since he was in the sixth standard. She was from a very conservative family, so she was not at all interested in love or anything like that. Despite repeated attempts from Aayush's side to win her over, she didn't budge from her stand. Aayush still loved her ever when it had been seven long years. Though he was trying to forget her, first love is something that haunts one throughout life. I knew that Aayush cried many times in solitude and that's why I wanted him to concentrate on somebody else. Now, after learning about Priya, I suspected that Aarti would never accept Aayush's proposal, if he ever proposed to her.

'She said nothing,' Aayush said.

'*NOTHING?* You mean, nothing? What do you exactly mean by *NOTHING*?'

'She just sat there and listened to what I had to say.'

'Oh, oh...I mean, that is strange. These girls, I tell you, are just impossible to understand,' I said loftily.

'That's why I am worried because she didn't respond the way I expected,' Aayush replied, looking really worried.

'Do you really like her?' I asked looking at him.

'I think so.'

'If you really like her, then there should not be any doubt in your mind about your feelings for her. When you are sure about yourself, then why don't you tell her?'

'I don't want to get hurt again and somewhere deep inside, I still love Priya.'

'I know it's difficult for you to forget her but...'

'Anshul, let's talk about something else,' Aayush said, interrupting me.

'Okay, how is Rajeev?'

'As usual, he is busy making inroads in the heart of Aarti,' Aayush smiled.

'He is really a competition for you, mate.'

'Nah, he is not.'

'Don't be so overconfident,' I said in a cautious tone.

'Don't worry about him. I know about him and I am playing my cards right,' Aayush said matter of factly.

'Oho, Mr Politician, all the best, then!' I said, grinning.

And we both laughed.

'Let's get back to the hostel,' Aayush suggested.

We turned back towards the hostel, when we caught a student run past us. 'Hey, why are you running? What happened?'

'*Result...result aa gaya.*'

'What? Where?' Aayush and I looked at each other, horrified. None of us wanted to believe what we had just heard; but we too started running. The internet lab was already bursting with first-year students. Everyone looked tense. In no time all our speculations were about to end. Some students were seen praying while others were looking intently at the computer screens. The rapidly changing expressions on their faces were telling their own story. We searched for a familiar face sitting in front of the computer screen and finally spotted Shubh.

'What happened? How much?'

'75.6 per cent.'

'Congratulations *yaar*. Can we see our result?'

'Yeah sure! Just tell me your roll number.'

First Aayush and then I blurted out our roll numbers while staring at the monitor with wide eyes.

'Aayush, you've got 73 per cent,' Shubh announced.

A broad smile came on Aayush's face.

'And Anshul you have scored 75.6 per cent.'

'Come again,' I said surprisingly.

'75.6 per cent,' he repeated.

Aayush and I hugged each other.

'Congrats, buddy,' Shubh was beaming.

'Thanks mate and same to you too.' I was really more than happy. 'And who topped in CS?' I asked.

'It's Avantika; she got 83.4 per cent,' Shubh replied with pride in his voice.

Well, who the hell has said life is fair? But I was happy for Aayush and myself.

9

The Accident

Everyone was either flattened or flattered by his or her results, but it was the result of Avantika that caught everyone's eye in CS. The faculty was quite impressed and so were the boys, but what had clicked for her were the feelings of some fellow girls for her.

* * * * *

'Congratulations,' Vineet said to Deepti, who was sitting in the sun, along with Saniya.

'For what?' Deepti asked, looking at Vineet.

'For scoring 80 per cent marks in the first semester. It undoubtedly calls for a treat,' Vineet said.

'79.9 per cent,' she corrected.

'Sorry!'

'It is 79.9 and not 80,' she said, searching for something on the marble floor.

'Okay, so what? It is only a matter of 0.1 per cent. But a

treat still remains to be given,' Vineet said, looking puzzled.

'I don't think so and why aren't you asking for a treat from Miss Avantika?' came the curt reply.

'Yeah, you are right. Some misers are born to be miserable. This time it is 0.1 per cent and if God listens to my prayers, next time it might be 10 per cent.'

'What do you mean?'

'Oh excuse me, I was not talking about you Miss 0.1 per cent,' Vineet said with contempt.

'Oho, someone is really angry,' Deepti said in a derisive tone.

'No, someone is jealous. Yeah, you were right. Avantika, I think, is better than you.'

'I am not jealous.'

'Oh really Miss 0.1 per cent?' it was Vineet who smirked this time.

'Don't call me that.'

'What, Miss 0.1 per cent?'

'Saniya let's go away from here,' Deepti said, while preparing to leave.

'You don't have to go anywhere. I am leaving.'

'No need to make excuses. We don't need your sympathy.'

'What excuses are you talking about?'

'About the very same excuses you made just now.'

'You think I am going from here because I have to go somewhere else for a treat or something?'

'I didn't say that.'

'But you did mean that,' Vineet said.

Tension was rising by the minute.

'No I was not.'

'You were.'

'Then why don't you sit down?'

'Only a moment ago somebody wanted me to leave.'

'And somebody was making excuses.'

'Where are you going?' Vineet asked on seeing Saniya's sudden movement.

'I need to go to the library. You guys can brawl till then and I hope by the time I come back, you both would have resolved your tussle,' Saniya smiled.

'Take your own time in the library; no need to hurry,' Vineet said, while looking at Deepti from the corner of his eyes.

'How much have you got?' Deepti continued.

'If you want me to go from here, then tell me straight away. Why make excuses?'

* * * * *

'Where are you going?' Eashaan asked Saniya after completing his 19th round from the canteen to the library.

'Nowhere; just looking for a place where I can spend some time till their fight gets over. So you were in the library?'

'Me in the library? Never a possibility. I was free, so I thought…you know,' Eashaan said as he gazed at the place where Vineet and Deepti sat.

'Uh, I understand,' Saniya said, looking at Eashaan.

'I am very tired and why don't we sit down?' Eashaan said while sitting down. Saniya joined him.

'Who is that boy?'

'Which one?' Eashaan asked absently.

'That boy in the half-sleeved sweater.'

'Huh…Oh that boy! He is Pawan. Why are you asking about him?'

'Nothing, I had heard that he is a very good singer,' Saniya replied, feeling embarrassed at her own answer although Eashaan didn't notice this as he was too preoccupied in his thoughts.

'Yeah, he is.'

'You like her a lot, don't you?'

'Who?' Now it was Eashaan's turn to go red in the face.

'You know who. It's written on your face.'

'Yes, I do but it doesn't matter when she is sitting there and me here. So who is in your family?'

'Papaji, Mom and two brothers. And yours?'

'My family is a joint one.'

* * * * *

The weather had become warm but not everyone was affected by it. The first semester results had caught many on their wrong foot. In any case I was surprised at my own results. It was a real shocker for me also but I didn't realise that it was such a kick in the teeth for many of my classmates and even some of the faculty members. Ms Barkha, whom, I mean, 'we' adored, even told me that she was not expecting anything like this from me. I couldn't figure out whether she was praising me or scoffing at me, so I took it on a positive note. Undoubtedly she was jeering at my ability to score good marks but somehow I couldn't get angry with her.

* * * * *

It was a relief for all of us to see the results declared but peace in my life still eluded me. Many a times I found Avantika staring at me as if searching for some traces of disappointment or guilt, but I was absolutely clear in my mind that I was not going to fall in the trap anymore. It was indeed not an easy task to ignore someone whom you saw every other day, but we both were doing it with full sincerity; at least I was. But as time passed, I found myself getting more and more distracted than in the past.

One day I called Avantika when she was seated with Mandakini outside the library.

'Avantika, I don't like the way you stare at me.'

'Well Anshul, as you might be aware, since we are in the same class, we are likely to stumble upon each other,' she answered with a crafty smile dancing on her lips.

'Avantika, I know that is simple logic but according to me, staring at someone is a completely different thing than just bumping into someone by accident. Now it is up to you to do whatever you wish, but I would appreciate it if you would stop it,' I said plainly and left.

But things didn't go down well as I expected. Next day when I was roaming with Aayush, Avantika came to me.

'I want to talk to you.'

'Hm...m...m, okay.'

'All that you said yesterday was wrong. I don't know where you got all those strange notions. I would request you to stop commenting on me,' she said in one breath.

'First thing, I don't have the habit of commenting on girls and more so if it is you. Secondly, if any of your so-called friend has told you that I had commented on you, then I am sorry about my comments. 'Bye,' I said and left.

'You are really impossible,' said Aayush to me on hearing about the whole incident.

* * * * *

One day, Vineet told Aayush and me that they were planning an outing on the following Monday and wanted to know if we were interested in joining them. They had planned to go and watch a movie in one of the better theatres of Bareilly. I was plainly not interested in torturing my seat by sitting on the nail-filled seats for three hours, but Aayush was eager to go. However, since I liked Vineet's and Shubh's company, I agreed to go. Apart from Shubh and Vineet, Vijay, Pawan, Priyank and Eashaan were also going. Although I was hardly friendly with any of them, I considered it a good opportunity to let down my hair. Except for Vijay, the rest of us were in CS while Vijay was in the Electronics branch. Vijay and Vineet were childhood friends, while Pawan and Shubh were in the same class since their early days. So the bond was already very strong between them and the only strangers in the group were Aayush and I.

* * * * *

On that fine Monday morning, we set out for the city in a tempo (a three-wheeler). It was a wet day with rain-drops sprinkled on the road since the previous night. It was still drizzling on and off. The tempo was already filled with five persons, contributing to a grand total of thirteen human bodies inside that steel cage with a capacity for eight. So Vineet decided to stand sideways with half his body hanging outside. However, it was our high spirits which made the tiresome journey a pleasure for we went joking and laughing at each other in that crammed little space. Shubh insisted on Vineet coming inside and after a few initial refusals, Vineet agreed. The tempo moved fairly briskly, although the traffic was at its usual peak. On one occassion, the tempo tried to overtake a vehicle from the wrong side and one of its rear tyres got off the road. I had watched this in movies but never experienced it. The tempo lost its balance and to one side turned. Due to the high speed, it started skidding on the road and produced sparks. In the flash of our eyelids, it left the boulevard and landed on the wet earth with a thud.

The tempo had turned sideways, blocking the door and caging a pack of human bodies. All of us started screaming at the top of our voices for help. It was a relief that nobody was hurt seriously, though I was proved wrong in no time. Since Aayush had been seated in the front on the driver's seat, hanging slightly outside, the entire weight of the tempo had rested on his left hand. The driver had already made a dash for his life. The feeling of getting trapped inside that steel body was awfully scary and for one moment I had felt that it was the death-knell for all of us. Our screaming however, drew a few people from the fields and they started lifting the vehicle. But it proved too heavy because of the weight inside. We started banging on the windows in an attempt to break the glass pane. At last, one of these loosened a bit and ultimately gave way to the outside world. One Sardarji, Vineet, Eashaan and Priyank, who were less dented than the others, soon jumped outside from that gap and started to help in lifting the vehicle. In next to no time, the vehicle was standing on its wheels.

The injuries were not trivial as I had expected. Aayush definitely had a fracture, while Shubh had injured his back and shoulders. My forehead was bleeding though I didn't feel any pain. Thankfully, Vineet, Vijay and Eashaan were not seriously injured. Some people helped Aayush and Shubh and gave them water to drink. Vijay helped me in washing the blood from my forehead. Each one of us was gnashing our teeth at the driver but he was nowhere to be seen. The only thing left as his legacy was his tempo, so the next move was to damage it to such an extent that it wouldn't be on the road for the rest of its life. In no time, the window panes were rolling on the dirt outside and soon the tempo began to look like the skeleton of a rickety contraption.

Twists never cease to surprise us. Here also, while we were cursing the driver, in a short period the people who had been helping us, turned hostile towards us. In a matter of seconds, the tables were turned and now we, who had been victims of a near-fatal accident a moment ago, were enemies of our own life-savers. Someone had whispered in their ears that the driver belonged to their community and since his tempo had been dismantled, they decided to take revenge by injuring us. Before we could even fathom the situation, sticks and bamboos were out. The Sardarji who was also with us in the tempo suggested that we should leave before the situation got out of hand. We promptly followed his advice by hiring a tempo to take us to the nearby hospital, which turned out to be the same hospital where I had donated my precious blood and which I now needed desperately.

* * * * *

Sitting in the lobby, I felt a sense of nostalgia engulf me. Aayush and Shubh were injured seriously and we all too were in need of medication. Everyone was quiet, I don't know why, but I was really in a state of shock and thus unable to say anything. That a day which had been planned so excitedly had turned into a nightmare, could not be imagined by anyone.

'Shit, shit! That driver should be damned to death,' Vineet said like a raging bull with anger flaring through his nostrils.

'If it had been my city, I would have really killed him,' Eashaan seconded him.

'Next time I see him, I'll really gonna bury that crook right there.'

'Please be quiet,' the nurse warned Vineet.

'Sorry, sister,' Pawan said and clutched Vineet's hand to quieten him down. It was however, a monumental task considering his temper.

Shubh had his dressings done while Aayush's was going on.

'Hey, the rest of you, come one by one for the dressings and injections,' announced the nurse, coming out from the emergency room. One by one each of us were wrapped in white band-aid, except for Eashaan and Vineet who were not so badly hurt.

Now the toughest part was to get back to the hostel without attracting attention, which was not easy.

Going towards the college seemed like walking on the longest road of my entire life. In the end, we reached the hostel and packed ourselves in Eashaan's room as it was the nearest room we could get into. After much discussion, we decided to fabricate the story that we all had met with a serious accident and not mention anything about being beaten up by our own well-wishers. However, one of the hostellers, who was going in a tempo had seen us being trodden on the road and had presumed it to be a case of eve-teasing for which we were getting manhandled. The news spread like wild fire and within seconds, before any of us could understand or explain anything, we were labelled as guys about whom every mother warns her girl in advance. So it all meant no chance of any girlfriends, no chance of getting good internal assessments and no chance of anything else.

A few did believe our side of the story, but most of them were sceptical.

* * * * *

It was hard to attend college with a bandage tied across the forehead and rumours flying high. Since we did not want to venture out alone, we decided to remain absent from college as long as possible. But it was easier to say and harder to bunk college in the first year, with Shubh, Pawan and Aayush on our side and who were known as guys who never missed any of the lectures, even in their dreams. Eashaan didn't have any major injury to show although some of his body parts pained; the wounds were not visible from outside. It pained him immensely that despite being one who had been actively involved in the accident, he was kept away from the rain of sympathy that greeted the others as he had no visible wound to attract sympathy. So he readily arranged for a small band-aid to apply on his forehead and use it under the supervision of Pawan.

It was really embarrassing for eight damaged guys to walk in a group from the hostel to the college without attracting attention. I felt as though time stood still and everyone in our vicinity had frozen to the spot to stand and stare at us. The only thing that moved was our feet. Each one of us could listen to our heartbeats and the worst part was that I felt as though mine would hump out through my mouth. I clenched my teeth tightly.

I glanced sideways and found Vineet babbling something which sounded like 'F*** yourself you as*****s.' Finally, after the longest journey of our lives, we reached the threshold of our class.

'Why are we all standing here? Get inside,' Shubh said from behind.

'I don't think it will be great idea,' Eashaan replied, glancing from Shubh to Vineet.

'What kind of crap is this? Move or let me go.'

We immediately moved sideways, making space for Shubh to enter inside.

'I didn't mean that I wanted to go inside. I meant to say that we all should go together,' Shubh said while taking a step backwards, as he didn't expect such swift action from so many disjointed bones.

'After your marriage also you will say the same thing that we all should go "inside" together,' Eashaan said with a mischievous smile.

Shubh looked at Eashaan with blazing eyes.

'I think Shubh is right,' Vineet said in a stern voice. We all stood in a queue and placed our right leg forward. I felt like a newly-wed bride entering her new house.

'Ch...h...h...h, ah...h...h...h, Omigawd,' whispered the girls in a sympathetic tone.

I felt a nice tinkling sensation in my head.

We all sat on the last bench to avoid any unnecessary questions about our accident.

'Are you guys alright?' Deepti asked Vineet and Eashaan.

'Yeah, I'm fine,' Vineet replied rather pleasantly.

'Me too,' Eashaan joined in the chorus.

'How did it happen?' Deepti asked with curiosity.

'Well, that's a long story. In a nutshell, I am alive and...' Eashaan kicked Vineet on his leg.

'...kicking,' Vineet completed.

'Well that's great,' Saniya said to Vineet. 'You don't

seem to be having many injuries as such.' She continued to look at Eashaan.

'What? You don't like me in one piece?' Eashaan asked, deeply hurt.

'No, I didn't mean that,' Saniya tried to clarify.

'You know I am hurt but I can't show you where because...' Eashaan said very sullenly.

'Actually his shoulder and back are hurt, but it's only because of him that I am seated in front of you,' Vineet interrupted Eashaan.

'Oh...h...h...h, how so?' Deepti asked intriguingly.

'That Eashaan will explain to you. Right now I have to go to the library,' Vineet stood up. 'Okay then, I will meet you later.'

'I also have some work in the library; I am also coming with you,' Deepti said in a casual tone, not knowing that it would spoil the whole play.

'Deepti, I was about to tell you that I had to renew my library card, so I will go with Vineet. Just tell me, which book do you want to get issued?' Saniya said, taking the matter in her hands.

'But...,' Deepti said, not a bit convinced.

'Well, I think she is not comfortable sitting here with me. There is no problem if she wants to go,' Eashaan played the last card and how correctly.

'No I didn't mean that. Okay Saniya, just check if they have any good novel of John Grisham's,' Deepti said finally. A large smile spread on Eashaan's face.

* * * * *

'Congratulations!'

I was startled at the voice that came from behind. 'I

don't understand,' I said on noticing Kruti's beaming face.

'You got 75.6 per cent, no?'

'Oh…h…h…h that! Thanks and congrats to you too. You are among the top five in the class,' I grinned.

'Thanks. How is your forehead?'

'Now it is better,' I replied carelessly as my head couldn't have been better.

Kruti was a girl of normal height with a slightly dark complexion that only imparted her the 'oomph' factor. Her hair was partially coloured and her black eyes revealed arrogance which only made her more desirable.

'Are we going to stand here or you are going to invite me for a treat?' she asked playfully.

'Oh…h…h…h…sure. What would you like to have?' I asked her.

The only thing that I was not sure of was the amount of money in my valet. I quickly searched my back pockets, then the side pockets and felt the rustling of paper in one of them.

'What happened? Why are you standing?' she asked, looking at me strangely.

'Nothing, absolutely nothing, let's go,' I said with a forced smile.

I glanced at the paper. It had a lonely ten printed on it. *What could ten bucks buy,* I debated in my mind. I began searching for any options.

'Cornetto; I want one Cornetto,' Kruti said excitedly, looking at me.

Well a ten couldn't buy something worth twenty – that was simple Mathematics. So it was out of the question.

'Well Cornetto, I mean it is wow, but I am not in the mood for ice-cream. But if you want, then you can have it,' I said looking for any clue on her face for the after-effect of my sentence.

'No, if you don't want, then we will have it some other time. In that case, juice will do,' she expressed another wish.

'One glass of juice costs 10 bucks,' I calculated mentally. *Well, at least that was affordable.*

She had already reached the counter as I planned on finding some other excuse.

'No fruits, hence no juice,' the boy at the counter replied.

'Oh....h...h...h no. Now what?' Kruti asked, looking rather depressed.

'I have an idea,' I said, my eyes shining bright. 'We can have a cold drink.'

'Yeah, that will be great,' Kruti said, sounding her usual self again.

'One glass of cold drink means five bucks,' I calculated and sounded pleased with my own idea.

'Two glasses of Fanta,' I ordered with utmost confidence.

'So Tina and you...' Kruti fired the question after settling down on a chair.

'Tina and me? What about us?' I felt I had just sat down on a bed of thorns.

'You both are a couple, right?'

'Hell no, we are just friends. I mean only friends. Nothing else,' I clarified.

'Oh, I thought that you both...you know everyone thinks the same. Anyways, leave it.'

'You don't trust anyone, right?' I asked.

'No, it's not like that, but why do you think so?' she looked at me with curiosity.

'Nothing...'

'No...no...tell me.'

That day how I wished that the cold drinks would never finish, although all good things have to come to an end and so that was that.

But one thing was for sure, I really like accidents. In fact we all do.

10

Setting the Table

'Hi Anshul, what were you doing?' Shyam asked when I opened the door after a series of unsuccessful hammering.

'Nothing, I was about to retire to bed,' I said, looking at the clock whose hour-hand was rock steady at 1 o'clock.

'I want to talk to you about something important.'

'Huh? Okay, we will talk about it in the morning. Till then have a good night and sweet dreams too,' I said while rubbing my eyes with a feigned yawn, thinking that he might understand that sleep was the top priority for me at that point of time.

'C'mon *yaar*, tomorrow is off. The entire night is left for you to sleep,' and with that he approached my chair.

I gave him a look of disgust but now nothing could be done.

'Vineet and you are good friends?'

'I don't know.'

'What do you mean?'

'I mean I don't know. Is this your important thing?' I asked in an exasperated voice.

'No man, obviously not,' Shyam defended himself. 'Well, I was thinking if we could hang out together as we all belong to the same caste...'

'Can you please come to the point and stop beating round the bush,' I snapped at him in the middle.

'Since the last few days, especially after that accident of yours, Shubh and Vineet are trying to get closer to Avantika and Mandakini.'

I kept staring at him with disgust, overlooking his sarcastic emphasis at the word "accident". Shyam had been suspicious since the first day as he felt there was something more than that was told.

'I think you can talk to them, especially Vineet, on my behalf because I don't want anyone to get hurt irrespective of what caste we belong to. You know, what I mean, don't you?' Shyam continued despite my glaring looks.

'Do you think I give a damn as to who Avantika talks or what Vineet or Shubh is doing in the class, or do you really consider that I would like to be a part of your scheme by any means?' I said, trying to control my anger.

'Don't get me wrong. I was just trying to say that I don't want to ruin the chance of losing a future friend in Vineet.'

'In that matter also I can't help you as I don't want to be dragged in this crap. Now can I sleep?' I finished.

'*Yaar*, what are you so cross about? It's okay if you don't want to speak. I just thought that being such good friends, we were entitled to seek some favours from each other. But still, it is perfectly alright,' he tried again in a last-ditch effort to make me join in.

I feigned another yawn that was real close to a genuine one. It could turn dangerous for me if we had continued any further.

'Okay if want to sleep, then goodnight. But think about what I said at least once.'

'Okay goodnight then,' I got up from my bed to close the door.

'Ahem...goodnight then,' Shyam said, getting up with a somewhat sullen face.

* * * * *

Eashaan's cell phone moved at its place. 'What were you doing?' flashed a text.

'Listening Bryan Adams. U?' went the reply.

'Thinking abt somthin.' It was Binny's turn.

'What?' Eashaan enquired.

'*TV pe 'Maine pyar Kiya' aa rahi hai*,' Binny replied.

'I'm missing you,' Eashaan sent another.

The sentiments were rising.

'Me 2,' Binny replied.

Eashaan dialled the number. The call was firmly rejected.

'Mom is sitting with me; can't talk now,' came the explanation.

'I wish that 2morro isn't off. I hate it when I can't see u at least once in the day,' message went.

'Come home for lunch 2morro. Mom will be happy to c u.' One new message received.

'Okay,' Eashaan replied.

'I'm missin u.'

'Me 2.'

'Goodnight, sweet dreams.' Eashaan put the phone by

his side, a broad smile dancing on his lips.

'Who is it?' he asked, as his smile took flight when he heard someone banging on the door.

'Daddy.'

'Whose Daddy?'

'Yours; now open the door.'

'Wait.'

'What?' Vineet asked, entering the room.

'What's what?' Eashaan hesitated.

'Why are you so happy?' Vineet knew he was on to something.

'Who, me? No, not at all.'

'So you talked to her.'

'Who?' Eashaan knew his efforts were futile.

'Deepti. What else can make you so happy?'

'She has invited me for lunch tomorrow at her home.'

'Good going,' Vineet patted him 'but hiding this from your Daddy, huh?'

'I was about to...'

'It's okay.'

'No really,' Eashaan stammered.

'I said it's okay,' Vineet said. 'Canteen?'

'Okay.'

'You will pay.'

'But last time also...' Eashaan stopped midway looking at Vineet's face. 'Okay.'

* * * * *

'What happened to you?' I asked, looking at Aayush's gloomy face. He was accompanied by Aarti.

'Nothing,' Aayush replied.

I looked at Aarti with a puzzled look.

'He like...'' Aarti said with a straight face. 'Payal.'

I looked at Aayush with amazement.

Payal was the skinniest girl anyone ever could be. If there was something called size zero, she was of size minus two. Being from a convent school, her tone and accent revealed a feeling of pride and arrogance.

'I don't think that she is by any means any good for you,' I said.

'But I only want friendship with her.'

'I think Anshul is correct; she is not your type,' said Aarti with determination in her voice, startling me.

'But I...'' Aayush protested.

'I don't know about you but one thing is for sure that she might not want to be your friend,' I said.

Aayush's mood remained the same and looking at him, my irritation rose.

'Aayush, she is not your type and she is flat too,' I said though regretting it the moment I uttered it. I tried to control my eyeballs from meeting those of Aarti, who, I felt, was staring at me.

'I wanted to tell you the same. She is not at all good for you,' Aarti complemented my feelings although in a low tone.

'Okay, I understand,' Aayush said, wanting to end this discussion as soon as possible.

The day when Aayush told me that "he *THINKS* he likes Aarti" flashed in my memory.

* * * * *

'Where have you been?' Shyam asked when I was about to reach the door of my beloved room for a nice retreat. He was standing near the stairs.

'Why?' I suddenly found my sleep at risk.

'I was searching for you for a while. Come to my room as I need to talk about something.'

'What's wrong with mine?' I asked.

'No it's important. We will talk in my room.'

"Crap!" I thought. 'Okay I am coming in a while,' I said.

It was a vicious circle in which I had landed, gladly though.

'What took you so long?' he fired, as soon as I entered his room. 'Do you know what happened today?' Unperturbed at my silence, he continued with his round of questions.

I kept on looking straight at him.

'Mandakini said that I am the only boy with whom she is comfortable when discussing anything and do you know she complimented me on my new hairstyle?'

I shifted my gaze from his messy hairstyle; it was nothing short of a disaster. But may be from a girl's point of view it seemed bearable or maybe even attractive.

'Shyam, I think you were right about Mandakini,' I said grinning. 'May be she likes you.'

'You really think so? I knew that you would believe me,' Shyam said excitedly.

'But I was thinking of one more thing,' I said, giving a small intentional pause.

'What's that?' Shyam seemed mildly worried.

'I think she feels you only consider her as your good friend and that you might never propose to her. Are you getting what I am trying to say? I mean, I think nobody has ever given her importance on account of her reserved nature and her underplayed beauty. I really feel you should tell her that you harbour the same emotions about her as she does for you,' I said between small pauses, with the breather working effectively.

'*Nahi yaar*, it's not possible.'

'Why? You think that she will reject your proposal?'

'May be yes or may be not, I don't know,' Shyam said hesitatingly.

'So, who is asking you to propose to her tomorrow itself? Take some more time. Observe her. You are the only boy in the college whom she talks to, so it will be easy for you to spend more time thinking over it.' I didn't want this moment of weakness to go in vain.

'I think you are right.'

'Well, this time I am,' I smiled.

When Shyam left, the table was set. The only question left was *when?*

11

A Shot of Truth

'You know, Anshul, Mandakini is prettier than Avantika. She is a bit chubbier than her but her looks, her face and skin tone is far better than Avantika's.'

'I don't know,' I said, looking into the darkness.

'What are you staring at?'

'That boat in the sea.'

'What? What are you saying? Cut out that bullshit,' Shyam said irritatingly.

After you, Your Highness, I thought, looking at him intently. 'Yeah, what were you saying about Mandakini?' I asked.

'I was saying that I am thinking of proposing to her.'

Suddenly my eyes sprang to life. 'What? Are you serious?' I asked just to check that I was not hearing voices in my head.

'Yeah.' That was the best affirmation I had ever got.

'When?'

'I don't know. I really don't know. Do you think I should give it some more time?' The confusion was surfacing again.

Crap, this is not going anywhere. It was again that vicious circle.

'Are you really sure about whatever you told me regarding her staring at you and all that stuff? Was it real?'

'One hundred per cent correct.'

'And anything that happened recently?'

'Only the things that I had told you that day,' Shyam said, being his usual self.

'I think that's great,' I said in an over-excited tone.

'She also keeps on staring at me for long durations.'

'Dude, I think this is the right time. Spardha is also right in the corner. You won't get a time like this,' I said in an encouraging tone.

Spardha was a national-level sports festival of our college in which eight to ten local college teams competed for medals when most were already reserved for GLSCET. As it was getting organised after an year, the seniors and us, both were equally excited to be a part of our first festival.

'Okay, let me figure it out for a while what I should say. Although I know the answer will be positive, but still I want to floor her with my proposal,' Shyam said after giving a small pause.

'You will definitely.'

'Thanks, buddy,' he grinned

'No need at all,' I smiled back (*was it wicked of me, I didn't know*). 'Okay, I am going then. You have a lot of work to do.'

* * * * *

"I declare Spardha open," the MD announced the start of my first sports festival. We wanted to see the opening ceremony, so Aayush and I had woken up at 6 o'clock on a holiday and were on the field in no time.

The opening soccer tie was about to start when I thought of taking another nap. Aayush was staying behind to cheer his favourite seniors who were playing in the team.

'Hey Anshul,' a soft voice stopped me on my way.

'Oh…h…h…h, hi,' a smile came to my face.

'Woke up so early?' Kruti asked.

'Yeah, I wanted to see the standard of the opening ceremony of our college. But how have you come so early?' I asked a little surprised. Kruti was a day scholar like many of the other girls of our college.

'One of the seniors told me yesterday that it was compulsory to come today; so I came.'

'God bless that senior,' I muttered under my breath.

'Are you saying something?' Kruti asked, looking at me in amazement.

'Nothing, I just wanted to know about your friends. Aren't they coming?'

'Actually they are, but I think they will be late. They sent me a message that they may get late. But I guess, it's okay now,' she beamed, looking at me.

'I didn't understand.'

'Were you going somewhere?'

'I was thinking of taking a nap,' I blurted out.

'Oh…h…h…h, I thought we could...anyways, forget it,' she sounded a bit disappointed.

'It's not a problem. We can sit together and wait for your friends to come,' I said, trying to undo the damage done.

'That is so sweet of you,' she said while sitting down on a dry patch of grass. I followed suit.

'Who else is coming today among the day scholars?' I asked, trying to sound casual.

'Whom do you want to come?' she asked playfully.

'Well, as a matter of fact, no one in particular,' I replied.

'About Tina I don't know, but other than her, Mandakini and Payal said that they will come,' she said with a tinge of sarcasm in her voice.

Mandakini is also coming. Then today is the day, I thought about Shyam.

'Hey, I am here. What are you thinking?' Kruti pulled me back from my thoughts.

'I was thinking that since Tina and I have a good rapport as others think and refer to us as a couple or something, after seeing us together today, I am afraid the same will be said for us,' I fired a killer.

'I don't have any problem with Tina or you. At least she is far better that Avantika,' Kruti retorted.

'I don't understand. What is your problem with Avantika?'

It was now getting interesting.

'I think Avantika doesn't deserve the spotlight she gets. She is just plastic in every sense – her way of talking, her walk, her behaviour, everything is artificial and fake.'

I couldn't stop myself from grinning.

'Anyways, why are we wasting time in discussing her?' she continued.

'How could I know?' I said playfully.

* * * * *

'Anshul,' someone called out my name.

'Ahem! Excuse me,' I excused myself from the company of Kruti.

'Today is the big day. Mandakini is alone and I think Avantika won't come for a while,' Shyam said, sounding ecstatic.

My eyes shone brightly. 'All the best dude, but I have to go right now.'

'Okay, we will sit there. That place is somewhat deserted and if Avantika comes, she won't be able to find us for some time,' Shyam said, pointing at one corner.

* * * * *

'You both are friends?' Kruti shot one, as soon as I returned.

'Somewhat. Why are you asking?' All of a sudden I found myself on the back foot.

'You strike friendship with anyone and everyone,' she shot another.

That's what I too was thinking, I thought.

* * * * *

'Hi, how come you are alone? Where is Avantika?' Shyam asked.

'She will take about an hour to reach here,' Mandakini replied. 'Well, someone is wearing a new shirt.'

'Thanks, I thought you won't notice. You are looking pretty too,' said Shyam, feeling a wave of confidence surge inside his body.

'Thank you very much for flattering me.'

'Let's sit there; the noise here is too much,' he suggested. Every step they took made his hands wet and heart beat faster.

'What's happened to you? Why are you sweating so much?' Mandakini asked while sitting down.

'Nothing, I am perfectly okay,' Shyam said, wiping the droplets of sweat from his forehead.

* * * * *

'What do you think of Saumya?' I asked, looking straight into the eyes of Kruti.

'Why? Is something going on in your mind?' Kruti asked.

'I was thinking of befriending her,' I still kept on looking into her eyes.

'Why are you asking me then?'

'Just like that.'

'I think she is not our type.'

'So who is my type? You?'

'Me? Obviously not,' she smiled cunningly.

'You don't trust anyone easily, right?'

'What makes you think so?' she said.

'I don't know, but you don't have many friends and you don't talk to many people out here.'

'Well, that's a personal choice. I don't think one needs to talk to everyone. And maybe you are right, but still I am talking to you.'

'And that is pretty strange.'

'And why is it so?'

* * * * *

'Is something bothering you?' Mandakini asked, looking rather worried.

'Actually, yes! I was thinking about something lately,' Shyam said as if he was having difficulty in uttering those words.

'You can tell me,' Mandakini tried to reassure him.

'Mandakini, I don't know since when I developed these feelings.'

'What kind of feelings? I don't understand,' Mandakini asked, placing her hand on his hand.

'I think I LOVE YOU,' and he blurted it out.

All of a sudden, the air stopped flowing. All the sounds disappeared. Everything froze in its place. A sensation of numbness engulfed both of them.

* * * * *

'......Because you are not my type either,' I said after a small pause.

'And who is your type?'

'I thought you knew it more than I do.'

'Still I want to hear it from you.' Kruti was now getting a bit anxious.

'That I will tell you some other time. Right now I have to leave,' I said, watching Shyam go towards the hostel at a swift pace.

'Where are you going?' Kruti asked, watching me get up.

'Oh…h…h…h, I am really sorry but I have something important to do. I have to go right now.'

'Okay, bye then.'

''Bye.'

* * * * *

'What does she consider herself? Is she a princess? *Kabhi sheesha dekha hai usne*? Who gave her the right to play with the emotions of others?' Shyam said, breathing heavily.

'What did she say?' I asked calmly.

* * * * *

'I don't...' Mandakini finally mustered all her energy to utter this before overcoming the shock.

'Mandakini, don't say anything. I know, you also like me. All those things you do for me without my asking for them are a testament of your love for me. I know you might not be aware of these feelings in yourself but if you delve deeper, you will find...' said Shyam at his usual best.

'I don't love you at all. I was really never interested in any of these things. I always considered you as a good friend and nothing else,' she poined out. He was almost on the verge of screaming.

'I know this is difficult for you to accept right now, but I know you love me and soon you will also realise it.'

'What? I really don't know from where you got all these weird notions. But the fact is that I DON'T LOVE YOU at all,' she said emphatically, trying hard to keep her head cool.

'But at the fresher's party, I saw you staring at me many a time; in the lab also you completed my work without my asking for you to do so and...' Shyam continued in a hurt tone.

'Fresher's? I don't remember anything like that and in the lab also, I only acted as a friend and nothing else.'

'But...'

'Shyam, I think we should leave this topic here only. It will be good for our friendship,' and so saying, she got up to signal the end of the discussion.

* * * * *

Shyam kept on saying a lot of things even after she had left, but I was in no mood to listen. I closed my eyes and the image of Avantika appeared in front of my eyes. Now Shyam and Avantika could never be together. I felt a dash of guilt but it vanished as soon as I turned my attention to Avantika's face.

'Anshul, it's a secret between the two of us. Please don't tell it to anyone,' Shyam pleaded, looking helpless.

'Don't worry, it will be a secret. I need to take a bath. I will meet you later,' I said and dashed for the door. I was afraid that I might appear too happy if I stayed a minute longer.

On my way to my room, I tried not to smile but I failed miserably.

* * * * *

Nothing lasts forever, not even the smell of victory and happiness.

As the new semester had started, news about Barkha ma'am leaving the college came as a shock. She had got engaged to some software engineer in Bangalore and was soon getting married. The news broke many a heart, including mine but that's what life is all about, I think.

This piece of news had a greater impact on some of the guys who even started behaving like lunatics.

* * * * *

'Hi,' Aayush greeted Payal, who was talking with her friends.

'Uh...hi...' she replied awkwardly.

'I am Aayush...uh...Aayush.'

'Sorry, but do I know you?'

'No, not actually, but we are in the same branch.'

'Oh, okay,' Payal said, still unsure about Aayush's existence.

'I WANT TO BE YOUR FRIEND,' Aayush finally mustered all his courage to utter.

'WHAT?' Payal spluttered out her shock in that single *WHAT*. 'Sorry, but I don't know you. I can't be really friends with you.'

'I just....' Aayush stopped midway. He looked sideways; people passed by, ignoring him completely. He again looked at Payal; she was still staring at him in disbelief. He quietly took a U-turn and started walking away.

The day was finished for him.

* * * * *

'I don't know what happened to me. I just don't know why I did it?' Aayush was shaking his head in disbelief.

Eashaan and Vineet were rolling on the floor, laughing uncontrollably.

'Stop it guys,' I said. 'I told you about her.'

'I know, but I don't know,' Aayush stuttered.

'What the hell are you muttering?'

Eashaan and Vineet's laughter grew louder.

'Did you tell Aarti about this?'

'No, but she will come to know. I just wish in the next semester she will not be in my class.'

'Who? Aarti?'

'No, Payal.'

* * * * *

The friendship between Tina and me was getting us nowhere. It was a mutual feeling that it really had started to stink. While most of my time was now divided between Aayush and others, Tina's attention was grabbed by a guy named Ronak. Soon he proposed to her and that marked the end of our friendship.

When one door closes, God opens many other doors. It was one of the lab sessions when I met Saumya. I think LAB stands for "Love and Beyond" as you get the perfect opportunity to hit on anything, be it girls even.

Saumya was unlike other girls; she was simply the simplest girl I had ever met, like the ones one reads about in fairy-tales. She was plump and perennially seemed petrified in a crowd. Her smile was genial but was rarely visible. Her eyes were large with an awkwardly twisted nose and bow-shaped lips. She was very polite and always answered all of my nonsensical questions with patience. In case of any difficulty, she tended to hide behind her bigger-sized friend, Meenakshi.

Meenakshi on the other hand, was taller, sharper and stronger than most of the boys in our stream. She was the only child of her parents and was given too many single-child habits like obesity, stubbornness, selfishness and short temper. Her hair were very long and her figure wayward. She didn't have any special features that needed any special mention, except for her strong aversion to me.

Every rose has a thorn and so it was also in my life.

12

The Indecent Proposal

Knock! Knock!

'Who is it?'

'It's me.'

'Sorry, but I didn't recognise you.'

'*Arrey yaar*, it's me, your second-year friend in GLSCET.'

'What? Are you serious?'

'Do I look like I am joking or something?'

'That means we are seniors now. Yahoooo!'

* * * * *

'What is that creature doing in Shubh's room?' I asked Aayush.

'Which creature?'

'The one who was lying on the bed?'

'Oh, he is Rajiv.'

'Oh…h…h…h...that same guy who wanted to adopt Aarti? I mean who is Aarti's distant neighbour.'

'Yeah, that same guy.'

'So he is the new roommate of Shubh and Pawan. Cool.'

Rajiv was almost 6 feet high and 3 feet broad with a physique of a bull and a nose like a waterfall as he suffered from a 24x7 running water-supply from his nose. He wore specs and ONLY specs on his extra large body apart from a Jockey innerwear. His favourite timepass was to brag about his cars and affluent cousins.

* * * * *

It had been a week since the new semester had begun and I found myself staring at the notice-board that reflected the divisions of students into the two sections of CS.

God please, no Avantika, no Shyam, I prayed silently.

'Hey which section have you got? Meenakshi and I got CS-1,' Saumya startled me with her comment.

'I was just trying to figure that out.'

'Hey, there you are,' she said pointing at the list.

'Oh yeah, thanks,' I said.

'Oh, so you are in CS-2,' I felt some disappointment in her voice or was that only a figment of my imagination?

'Crap!' I spitted.

'Why? What happened?'

'Nothing,' I hastily replied, hiding my disappointment on finding Avantika and Shyam in the same list.

'Look, Aayush is also in CS-1.'

'Aayush is in CS-1?' I looked closely and found that only Pawan and Aayush were in CS-1, unlike the rest of us.

* * * * *

The shuffling of the students had caused tremendous pain

and anxiety in some. Whatever the sections we were in, but we had to face each other for the next three years.

'Hi,' Deepti greeted.

'Hi,' Vineet replied with a sullen face.

'You are looking distressed?'

'Maybe there is some problem with your eyes.'

'I think someone is in a very bad mood.'

'Why are you worried about my mood?'

'Because we are friends and I want my friends to be free from all worries when I am happy.'

'And may I know the reason for your happiness?'

'Both Saniya and I are in CS-1, but why are you so angry? Avantika is in your class, right?'

'So what?'

'I mean you like her, right?'

'Actually you are right. Why am I feeling sad? Avantika and I are in the same class. I should be happy. Now I don't have to explain to you everything about our conversation... Gee, why I never thought about it?' Vineet said sarcastically.

'I never asked for explanations; it's you who gave them.'

'Oh, really! Then here is my last explanation. You know I think Avantika is a far better girl than anyone else here – she is smart, she is intelligent and she is also good looking,' Vineet's temper kept on rising.

'If you really think so, then what are you doing here? You should be with Avantika,' Deepti replied tersely.

'You really don't deserve a friend like me.'

'I only wish the best for you and your new friend.'

'Go to hell,' Vineet flared.

* * * * *

'It's all because of him that she is flying so high," said Vineet, still boiling with rage.

'Who is flying so high?' Shubh asked. Pawan shifted carelessly on his bed.

'That whore Deepti, all because of that dog Eashaan and...'

'Well said,' remarked Pawan.

'What happened?' Shubh asked tentatively.

Vineet told him about what had happened.

'I told you that she is jealous of Avantika,' Shubh felt a gush of fury.

'Here comes another Romeo,' Pawan laughed.

'Shut up Pawan,' said both Shubh and Vineet in unison.

* * * * *

'Hi, Kruti! Where have you been all this time?'

'Me or you? After getting into CS-2, you have almost forgotten your old friends.'

'Oh, really!'

'So, where are you going?'

'Nowhere, just weighing my options as to whether I should attend the tutorial today or not?' I said. 'What is your last lecture?'

'I think it's free.

"Okay, meet you then.' I was definitely thinking but not about the tutorial; rather I was mulling over spending time with Saumya. But being with her meant I also had to tolerate Meenakshi and that did not augur well for my health. In any case, Kruti was not a good option if one had to spend more than fifteen minutes with her.

* * * * *

‘Hi, I think you are free?’ I asked Saumya, who was looking pretty even at the last hour of the day.

‘You again bunked your tute!’ Meenakshi exclaimed. Saumya merely smiled.

‘Yeah, actually I don’t feel that attending tutorials will help in my cerebral augmentation.’

‘What segmentation?’ Meenakshi asked with her mouth wide open, enough to swallow the whole Pluto in one go.

‘Hey, this class is empty, we can sit here,’ I suggested, ignoring her non-cerebral questions.

‘Last time also you had bunked the same tutorial?’

‘And last to last also; now stop counting. I know you have a good memory.’

‘May we know why?’

‘No you can’t.’

‘Then we must leave you on your own to wander here and there.’

‘I had already told you the reason and apart from that, this is the only lecture when you are free.’

‘Don’t try to flirt with me.’

‘I am not trying; I am actually doing it,’ I said.

‘Forget it, men are really dogs.’

‘Your father is also a man.’

‘What did you say?’

‘Nothing.’

‘I am going to have some water,’ Meenakshi announced before leaving the room.

‘Hey look, I had put *mehndi* on my hands,’ Saumya exclaimed.

‘Good, is there something special today?’

‘I like its colour and smell. Why are you looking at my hands with such concentration?’

'I had heard that girls put the first letter of the boy's name whom they love, so I was searching for an "A",' I said, looking at her palms.

'Is…sh…h…h, you are really too much. I am going to have some water,' Saumya said, her face growing red with embarrassment.

'Hey, where are you going?' Meenakshi asked, while entering the class.

'Water.'

'Shall I join you?'

'No, its okay,' Saumya rushed outside.

* * * * *

'Wht you doing?' Eashaan sent a message in his SMS lingo.

'Nothin; just staring at stars,' Deepti replied.

'Did you find anything?'

'Yeah!'

'What?'

'Someone's smiling face.'

'Who's face?' Eashaan asked.

'The weather is getting so romantic, hope we cud be 2gether.'

'Me or him? Who is lurking behind the stars?' Eashaan sent another text.

'Jealous? Okay, vl tel u 2morro whose face it was.'

'Okay, see u in the recess.'

'Missin u, my *jahapanah.*'

'Missin u 2,' Eashaan pressed tne sent key.

'So whose face it was?' Eashaan and Deepti were sitting in the classroom.

'Which face?' Deepti teased him. 'Okay, okay, it was

somewhat like yours.'

'What do you think we are?'

'What do you mean? I don't understand?'

'I mean what is the status of our relationship?'

'We are friends, right?'

'You mean just like everyone else?'

Deepti remained silent.

'So you do the same kind of messaging with every other guy who is your friend as you do it with me?' Eashaan continued. 'What do you think I am?'

'You are a very special friend of mine. But Mom says that I should marry a guy with a stable job and not some businessman.'

'I am not concerned about what your Mom opines about me. I want to know, what do you think?'

'I mean, what Mom says is for my good only, so I think she is correct this time also,' Deepti responded, looking sideways. 'Where are you going?'

'I am feeling sick here,' he said and left without waiting for Deepti's reaction.

* * * * *

Somewhere else also the tussle for Lady Luck was heating up.

'Yesterday, Rajiv proposed to Aarti.'

'That's great. What did she say?'

'She said that she needed some time.'

'Really?' I was shocked.

'That means she might say yes. The girl is having the time of her life – getting pampered by two boys at the same time. That's cool, man.'

'Curb your observations, Anshul. Tell me what should I do?'

'Do you really love her?'

'What kind of a question is that?'

'I mean do you really love her, or do you think that you love her, or is it that because Rajiv is your competitor, you want her?'

'I love her, *yaar.*' My thoughts drifted towards Aayush's childhood love for the last eight years where he had never been able to convey his feelings but still kept her photo in his valet close to his heart 24 x 7.

'Why don't you ask her directly what she thinks about you?'

'It is not that easy.'

'It is also not that difficult. Look, she already knows that you like her. Then what is the problem? At least you will be free from these worries.'

'I don't know. I need some time.'

'*Der naa ho jaaye, kahin der naa ho jaaye*, my friend.'

* * * * *

'Hey are you coming in at the time of recess?' Meenakshi asked me.

'For what?'

'Today is Raksha Bandhan, you remember?'

'Yeah, I know,' I felt a bit scared.

'So, in the recess I will tie *rakhi* to my sweet brother, Shubh and guess what? Saumya too is planning to tie the *rakhi* on someone.'

'May I know who is that someone?' I asked though an uneasy tension gripped me.

'It is a surprise. So you are coming, right?'

'Yeah, I will try but I am not certain.'

'Please come.'

Saumya was lurking somewhere in the background. I looked at her. She was looking very cute today with a red *teeka* on her forehead. She was staring at me with her big black eyes. *No one could say no to those eyes,* I thought. I nodded my head in affirmation.

'Thank you,' she said.

'Okay, see you in the recess,' Meenakshi said.

If God wanted me to be her brother, then there was nothing I could do. But if she tied on me a *rakhi*, then, oh my God, please don't do this to me, I prayed desperately.

I cursed that person who initiated this *rakhi* ritual, though it was a bit late in the day. I alone couldn't have discontinued with this tradition of *rakhi* between brothers and sisters.

I reached a bit late to be able to gauge the situation. Meenakshi was beaming with pride while looking at Shubh. 'Hey look, it is looking cute, *naa*?' Saumya asked, pointing at Shubh's hand where a golden coloured thread was tied.

I nodded my head with a sinking feeling.

'Now it's my turn,' Saumya said with excitement. My heart began to beat violently; no, it began to thud loudly.

'Come and sit here,' Saumya suggested, looking at me. An image flashed in my mind of my school days when one of the hottest girls of our class nipped my emotions and feelings with a same kind of thread in front of everyone. I waited anxiously, fearing the end of my emotions.

'Anshul, move aside,' a voice announced behind my back, catching me unawares. I stood aside as instructed.

'Can you do it fast? I don't have time,' Vineet said in his usual tone.

'Shut up, this is not some cigarette that you can finish it in two drags. Be patient,' Meenakshi said.

Saumya tied the *rakhi* she had brought on Vineet's right hand. I smiled, looking at them.

'I think the lecture is going to start soon. We all should go,' Shubh suggested.

* * * * *

'Nice *rakhi*,' Avantika beamed at Shubh.

'Thanks.'

'Your sisters sent them?'

'Yeah, this one, but this one is from Meenakshi.'

Avantika looked puzzled.

'She is in CS-1.'

'Oh okay. Is she your real sister?'

'No.'

'What did you give her as a return gift?'

'Nothing yet, but I am planning to get her something.'

'I got a new suit in return from my brother.'

Shubh was awestruck by the beauty sitting in front of him.

'It is good to have such relations in a new place,' Avantika continued.

Shubh felt a bit apprehensive at her comments. He definitely didn't want any other sister in this new place.

'Who tied this *rakhi*?' Avantika asked, doing all the talking to Vineet.

'Saumya.'

'Oh…h…h…h, great. We catch the college bus from the same stop. She is a nice girl.'

What the bus had to do with *rakhi*, Shubh could not fathom.

'Vineet, let's go outside for some water,' Shubh said.

'Okay,' Vineet stood up. 'What happened?' Vineet asked suspiciously, coming out of the lab.

'Nothing as such. So what about you and Deepti? Still not wanting to talk to her?'

'Why should I always go? It's always me who apologises, but this time I am not going to feed her ego,' Vineet said, obviously wanting a change of topic.

'It's been quite long; let's go back to the lab,' Shubh said after a small pause.

* * * * *

Vineet's birthday was approaching and a surprise booze party was planned by Pawan, Eashaan and Shubh.

The clock's needle struck 12 at midnight and numerous bumps were given to Vineet. A birthday in the hostel is a day when even the greatest don of the college becomes a punching bag who enjoys being punched.

'Who is the hamper?' Pawan asked.

'Ask the birthday boy,' someone from the crowd shouted.

'Shubh, Vijay and Eashaan are my three hampers,' pat came the reply.

Without any prior notice, the wanted men were caught by innumerable hands of my tormentors and within seconds around twenty pairs of legs were searching for some space for their bums. This programme went on for almost fifteen minutes in which a number of futile attempts were made to escape and then rained a plethora of hugs and wishes upon Vineet, from both the seniors and classmates alike.

'Get Vineet in my room,' Shubh instructed Eashaan, who was still rubbing his butt.

'Vineet, let's go to Shubh's room for some fun,' suggested Eashaan, wrapping his hand around Vineet.

'HAPPY BIRTHDAY, VINEET,' we all shouted as he entered the room.

We all took our glasses, filled them with either whisky or Coke as per our choice, and raised a toast for his long life full of sex and loads of girlfriends.

Glasses after glasses kept on getting emptied and filled instantly. It was like a never-ending stream of *daaru* flowing from the bottles. With each successive peg, each of us tried to prove who was the biggest booze hound in the group.

'You know what? You are my best friends, but I don't deserve this. I am good for nothing,' said Vineet unexpectedly. We all were shocked to see tears roll down from Vineet's eyes. Pawan looked at Vineet with his eyes half closed.

'Hey buddy, don't cry. You are my best friend. You are really the best in this whole world,' Aayush said, patting Vineet's back. I felt like checking Aayush's glass which seemed to be filled with Coke.

'No, I am not. If I would have been, then I might have told her about my feelings.'

Aayush, Shubh and I were all taken aback at the mention of "*her*" in Vineet's life as all were heavily drunk. Luckily enough the Coke in our glasses couldn't have that effect despite a lot of overeactions from our side.

'Vineet, don't worry, she will be yours. Just don't cry,' Pawan wrapped himself around Vineet and planted a kiss on his cheek.

Two drunkards do make a merry couple, I thought.

'No she won't, because more than her, I love HIM.'

Oh shit, Vineet is gay. Aayush looked at me with the same

shocked expression that was visible on Shubh's face.

'Don't worry, he will also be yours,' Pawan planted another.

Crap, Pawan is also gay? I thought.

I glanced at Eashaan, Vijay and Rajiv who were piled on each other, having a goodnight siesta.

'You are such a good friend, Pawan, but I don't want to hurt him.'

'No one is going to be hurt,' Shubh told Vineet.

'Thanks, oops,' Vineet jumped as Pawan fell flat on the bed.

'Tell me *naa* that she will be mine.'

'Yeah, she will be yours,' Shubh assured him.

'I know you are with me. I love you DEEPTI, I love you Deepti,' he muttered before he also dozed off. Shubh looked as horror-struck as Aayush and I. We looked at each other. The party was over but not the heartaches.

* * * * *

There is nothing that a person can do if his luck is written with...., anyways forget it.

It was a normal day; a day which had nothing special about it, absolutely nothing. Meenakshi was sitting with Saumya on the stairs near their class. That was the exact position where I saw them when I went to meet Saumya (not Meenakshi, of course) during the recess.

'What has happened to you? Cold?' I asked, looking at Saumya.

'Hm…m…m…m!' Saumya replied with an almost cuddly look on her round face.

'I have some work to do; I am going to the class,'

Meenakshi intervened before leaving us alone.

'I think we should go somewhere else. This place is so crowded,' I said, fearing that Meenakshi might come back again to disturb us.

'Okay,' Saumya said, giving me a smile. Soon we were standing at a window in a deserted corridor. 'So, why are we here?' Saumya asked.

'Nothing, just...," I felt my ears getting red.

'Okay, as you say,' she started looking outside the window.

'Saumya, actually I wanted to ask you one thing but I am afraid you might get angry.'

'Ask *yaar*, after all we are friends,' Saumya smiled encouragingly.

Oh God, why do girls smile so nicely!

'I think you have been ignoring me for the past few days,' I said, looking at her for a positive response. She was looking at me with a child-like curiosity. 'Saumya, I really felt it strongly because I have begun to like you.' Her expressions changed from curiosity to shock. 'And I think that deep inside your heart, you also like me.' I was amazed that I could declare so much so blatantly. 'And I want you to know that even if my perception were to be wrong, I would like to be your friend just as we are now,' I said, pausing for a moment to see her response.

'You like Kruti, don't you?' she asked unflinchingly.

'No, she is just a friend.'

'But, I have heard from others that you like her.'

'Well then, that is also news for me.'

'Everyone says you are a big flirt and I also feel the same about you. Also everyone says that you are not trustworthy.'

'Well yes, I like to flirt but whether I am trustworthy or not, you have to decide on your own.'

'Why do you like me?'

'I don't know.'

'Even if I say no, we will be friends.'

'I hope so. See Saumya, you can take as much time as you wish to decide.'

She didn't say anything but kept looking at me with open curiosity. 'Okay,' she said after about 600 seconds that seemed like ages to me.

Then she asked as many things as she could in those 10 minutes which were left before the recess was to get over. 'I think we should go. Meenakshi must be waiting for me,' she said finally.

'Can you tell me what you think about me?' I asked as we began to part.

'I think that I like you,' she said smilingly.

I was both confused and happy.

* * * * *

Lying on the bed that night, it hit me like a lightning bolt. *Crap, she had said yes to me. That meant now no more flirting, no more intimacy with other girls, numerous questions, a lot of explanations without forgetting a truckload of expectations and if she got serious about this, then I would be in real serious trouble. Oh God what had I done? Oh how could I commit this blunder? Why the hell did I do it? Should I go and tell her that it was a mistake, that I miscalculated somewhere, somehow. May be I should tell her that I was drunk or maybe I was a mental, who had gone off course. I really was a mental case, else why would I tell her that? May be I was only dreaming and nothing had ever happened. Yeah, that's correct, I was only dreaming and it was my worst nightmare.*

I didn't know when I dozed off, thinking all these things but when I woke up, a wave of fear gripped me as soon as I opened my eyes. Sometimes nightmares do come true and I experienced this in the first break itself when I received a warm smile from Saumya and the most livid glare from Meenakshi. Previously the same smile brought a cheer to my face but now I felt duped by this smile. I gave a wary smile in return but took it back as soon as it had served its purpose.

'Gotta go. See you in recess,' I said hastily.

* * * * *

We were sitting in a deserted class. I was thinking very hard how to update her database with my lovey-dovey feelings. She was seated in front of me, looking very fetching with an extra line of *kaajal* in her large deer-like eyes and her hand placed carelessly on the table. I was staring at her hand where her blue veins were clearly visible due to her unusually fair hands. *Should I hold her hand or let it rest where it was?* I thought. My mind was wandering aimlessly. What should I do? Should I tell her or wait for some more time. She might come to know it eventually.

'What are you thinking?'

'What I am thinking I myself don't know,' I said, still looking at her hand instead of looking at her face. I was struggling every minute to undo my mistake. What was happening to me was beyond my imagination. I never imagined that some girl sitting in front of me would one day be my girlfriend. I was behaving very strangely. I shouldn't have done this and told her everything by now. My mind was pounding hard. 'Saumya, I want to say something to you,' I said after some time. She was looking at me intently. 'Saumya, look...'

She shifted her hand a bit. I measured the distance between her hand and mine. At that moment something unusual happened – she put her hand on mine and I felt an unusual sensation in my body. It was completely natural like it was always meant to be like that. All my anxieties and worries flew out through my ears for a few moments. Was it that simple? I think it was, but it was only I who was making it so complicated. And then we just looked into each other's eyes. And then there was the first of the many forthcoming best conversations of my life.

13

The Beauty and the Blood

'She has accepted my proposal.'

'Who?'

'*Arrey yaar*...Aarti,' Aayush said excitedly.

'That is great news. When did it happen? I mean, how did you propose to her?'

He told me about every nut and bolt of his triumph while I wondered whether I should tell him about Saumya and myself or should I wait? Finally I decided to wait.

* * * * *

'It won't work; this relationship is not going to work. Mark my words, this is the biggest mistake of your life. He is a complete jerk. Trusting him is like trusting a tiger which will treat you only as a food item. It will last only two to three weeks at the maximum.'

'But, he is good at heart.'

'How do you know? You are still a kid; anyone can con

you. At least you should have consulted me. What was the need of saying yes then and there?'

'I know I had hurt you but I know one thing for sure that when Anshul is serious towards someone, that girl would be the last girl in his life,' Saumya said, defending herself.

'And if that girl is not you, then? How can you be so dumb, believing all this crap?' Meenakshi asked acidly.

* * * * *

While some hearts were beating for each other, some others were trying to beat the hell out of each other. The vacuum created in the lives of Mandakini and Avantika due to the rift with Shyam was now filled by Shubh and Vineet. Shubh was happy that he had finally been able to create inroads into Avantika's mind and Vineet became his guardian angel.

This increasing proximity hurt Shyam no end and he finally decided to confront Vineet. The conversation that began as a regular chit-chat soon turned into a heated argument with both of them rolling on the floor and trying to punch each other as hard as possible. Fortunately, Ahmed, one of our classmates and I were witness to this battle and had to stop that cat fight by throwing one of them out of the room.

The next day the whole college was talking about the fight whose cause was apparently attributed to Avantika. Questions and comments kept on flying from every nook and corner of the college. Shyam was busy describing his heroics to anyone and everyone who was willing to lend him an ear while Vineet was, as usual, unreachable for any comments. So the only person who was accessible was yours truly whose favourite answer was, 'I have no idea what you are talking about.'

Two persons asked me this question very intriguingly – Saumya and Kruti. My reply gave them some reassurance that whatever they already knew was correct to the core.

This fight had undoubtedly benefitted one person and it is not difficult to guess who it was. It sealed the coffin of the friendship between Shyam, Mandakini and Avantika and buried it deep inside the history of the 2004 batch of students.

* * * * *

The turbulence was not there only in Shyam's life, but Meenakshi too was feeling the pangs of separation and desperation. With my entry in Saumya's life, Meenakshi now had to share Saumya's attention which previously was her sole right. Apart from that, the girl she disliked most was at the top of her brother's list of most desired persons. That directly implied that she had to bear innumerable hours just listening about Avantika. This aspect of her anger was also directed at on me with frowns and disgusted looks and sometimes with tantrums and taunts.

'I don't know why she hates me so much.'

'She doesn't hate you.'

'Then maybe it's her face that gives me an impression of a raging bull.'

'Why do you always make fun of her?'

'Because she chooses it to be that way.'

'I think you should talk more to her.'

'Look Saumya, we hardly meet each other for about half an hour on an average and if you want that out of those 30 minutes, I waste twenty minutes on Meenakshi, then you should seriously think again and I don't know what her problem is? If she can't give you thirty minutes from eight hours of your college life, then I really think she must visit some gynaecologist for her check-up because she might be a lesbian.'

'Sh…h…h…h, she is coming. Try to behave nicely,' Saumya whispered.

'So you are still here?' Meenakshi taunted.

'Yeah, and that too despite your displeasure.'

'I am not displeased about you being here.'

'Oh really? Then I think you are not a very good actor or you are a good liar. Anyways, I was just about to leave. 'Bye Saumya.'

'What does he think of himself?' Meenakshi frowned.

'Where have you been?' Saumya tried to change the topic.

'I was with Saniya and Deepti, but then they went to the library and unfortunately, I have to come here to spoil your party.'

'Meenakshi, why are you so prickly?' Saumya asked.

'I just don't like the sight of him.'

'Yeah, he also says the same about you,' Saumya muttered under her breath.

'You said something?'

'Nah...nothing.'

'How can you...?'

'Saumya, have you seen Anshul?' Aayush's terrified voice interrupted Meenakshi's sentence.

'He just left for the hostel. Why, what happened?'

'Nothing. If you see him, then tell him to meet me A.S.A.P.'

'Okay, but what has happened? Anything serious?' Saumya's questions echoed but Aayush was not there to answer them.

'Anshul…Anshul...'

He found me near the canteen.

'What has happened?' I shouted back.

'Come fast,' Aayush shouted.

'What happened?' I repeated my question while trying to match my pace with Aayush's.

'See for yourself.'

We reached the threshold of Shubh's room. A premonition that something serious had happened to Shubh gripped me. The room was already packed with friends. Pawan stood near the window. Shubh and Eashaan were seated on the bed. Vineet stood with his hands on his waist and looking ready to explode at a moment's notice. Vijay also stood leaning against another wall. The atmosphere in the room was grim and edgy.

'Close the door,' Vineet ordered.

I latched the door.

'Are you going to speak something or not?' Vineet bellowed.

'I am sorry.'

Eashaan's right hand was wrapped heavily in a bandage. A few drops of blood were visible on the white shirt.

'I am not here to hear your apology. Why the hell did you do it?'

Eashaan remained quiet.

'Do you understand how serious this matter is now? How can you be such a moron? Tell me, is it for that whore you broke that window?'

Eashaan winced with pain.

'I am okay now,' he said slowly.

'That we know, you idiot. What did she say to you?'

Vineet was not in a mood to stop.

'She said we are just friends, but then what about all those messages she sent to me? I felt like slapping her in front of everyone, but I can't. It was so frustrating. I didn't know what to do,' Eashaan said in one go.

Everyone was struck dumb. Shubh was looking really worried and staring at Eashaan's injured hand. Pawan continued looking outside the window, lost in his thoughts. Aayush seemed shattered.

'Okay, now that all have vented their frustration one way or other, I think it's time for us to leave. Shubh, c'mon, lift your bums. Vineet c'mon move,' Vijay said.

'This is really...' Shubh began to say something but stopped.

'You take rest,' I said, patting Eashaan's shoulder.

He looked at me with a blank expression. A triangle was formed on his shirt by three blood droplets. I left the room with mixed feelings.

* * * * *

'Yesterday, Deepti was crying bitterly,' Saumya said, while eating her lunch.

Sometimes I have felt that Saumya was capable of digesting any problem with her *rajma*-rice.

'And why was she weeping? She is such a clever bitch.'

'Anshul!' Saumya screamed, looking at me with disgust and leaving aside her favourite *rajma*-rice. 'She is my friend and it was not her fault.'

'Okay, okay, I am not saying anything about your friend but tell me one thing – since when has she become your friend?'

'I mean she is Meenakshi's friend, so she is mine.'

'Oh great, so what do you think? Did Deepti like Eashaan?'

'Nah, she considered him only as a good friend and that too not any more.'

'Why do you think that she can't like him or doesn't like him?'

'Well, you know, Eashaan is that kind of a boy and she is a simple girl with simple needs.'

I smiled at Saumya's naiveté while she was engrossed in her food.

'Hey guys, what are you doing? Going to hug each other?'

'Sorry to disappoint you, but not now,' I smiled at Saniya's sudden entry.

'Do you know where Eashaan is?'

'Sorry, but I have no idea.'

'Okay then 'bye,' and she left.

'Strange,' I said to myself.

'What?'

'Nothing,' I said promptly.

* * * * *

I reached just on time that day. It was cold and chilly outside. Everyone was preoccupied with the preparations for the forthcoming semester exams.

'Hi, you are looking pretty today,' I said in my usual tone when I met Saumya after the second lecture. Although every day I complimented her about her looks, the reality was that day she really was looking good.

She looked at me with some strange expression and a strange smile.

'Hi, Saumya,' Aayush came in.

'Hi.'

'And yes, a happy birthday to you!'

'Birthday? Today? What is the date today? Aayush knew it but how could I forget the date?' I literally felt the ground shake under my feet.

'Thanks.'

'Happy birthday, Saumya. Sorry I forgot...' I should not have said it.

She gave me the coldest of her looks.

How does it feel when you forget the first birthday of your girlfriend since the time she has entered your life? Well, it was horrible and proved rather expensive. It took me full three hours to convince Saumya that I loved her but such mistakes do happen once in a while.

* * * * *

The exams arrived followed soon by holidays.

The problem with having a girlfriend is that there is a lot of extra monetary burden on the lean shoulders of an unemployed, dependent, good-for-nothing and perpetually empty-pocket guy. However, my frugal nature (frugal because I don't like to call myself a miser or a money-enamoured demon) never caused a rift between Saumya and me. She knew about my empty wallet and also our decision to avoid being seen in public places without the company of a third person, and hence we never went to the canteen together during the entire second year.

Meenakshi's birthday was coming and she invited Aayush, Eashaan, Vineet, Shubh and surprisingly Anshul (I suspect Saumya was behind it). I felt petrified from inside firstly because a birthday meant I had to give some gift and for that one needed money and secondly because of my unusual experiences in the first year.

Eashaan, Vineet and I decided to share the cost of a gift among ourselves. Shubh and Aayush chose to give a separate gift because Shubh was the brother and because Aayush was a dude.

We reached at 11:30 just to ensure that we would not miss the cake and food. Moreover for Vineet and me, the RG (return gift) was very important.

We found ourselves sitting in a small, cosy room with Meenakshi's Mom looking at us intently. I immersed myself in a newspaper.

'Water anyone?'

'Thanks,' Shubh said.

I looked up causally and saw a beautiful girl standing with a tray of glasses.

'Who is she?' Eashaan asked me.

'I think I know her,' I smiled.

'You are looking different,' Vineet said.

'Is that a compliment? Saumya asked.

'I will tell you that later.'

Saumya's orange suit was looking tailor-made to enhance her looks. The makeup was at its minimal. There was a natural glow in her open smile and this was attracting everyone's attention.

'Hi everyone,' Saniya exclaimed from the door.

'Hi,' Eashaan replied, looking pleased.

'Where is Deepti?' Vineet asked.

Shubh, Aayush and I looked at each other.

'Well I am afraid to say she won't be able to come due to some urgent work at home,' Saniya said.

'Well nothing can be better than this. She doesn't deserve to be here,' Vineet said acidly.

I was confused at the kind of love Vineet shared with Deepti.

'Saumya, why are you standing? Take a chair and sit down,' Aunty said. '*Aaj hamari Meenakshi ne poora khana apne aap banaya hai.* Although I kept telling her that there was no need, but she didn't allow me to do anything in the kitchen except to help her a bit.' She looked at Meenakshi, who stood next to her, looking bloated with pride.

'So you know cooking also?' Vineet commented.

'*Jee haan.*'

'I thought you only thought about books and ways to irritate me.'

I looked at Saumya. She glanced at me and withdrew her glance promptly.

'*Beta, hum to kitna kehte hain ki "Padhai-likhai pe dhyan lagao.* This cooking-shooking you can learn anytime." But she is just like her father. He too is very passionate about good food.'

'*Ji auntyji, woh to dikhta hai,*' Vineet said, looking at Meenakshi.

'I don't know how she gets so many marks even though she doesn't study at all,' Aunty continued, overlooking the sarcasm in Vineet's voice.

I snorted at the remark. 'Aunty, some people are gifted,' I said looking at Aayush.

'Okay, why don't we all head towards the dining table?' Meenakshi interrupted.

After four hours of non-stop *Meenakshi-Purana*, a few silly fights and lot of good food, we dispersed.

My idea of a perfect day had been fulfilled.

'Is there something going on between Saumya and you?' Vineet asked me as we waited for an auto. His words penetrated my mind and thoughts like a bullet.

'No. Why?' I stuttered.

'Nothing, just felt like asking,' he said, looking at the traffic. My palms became sweaty and I kept looking eagerly for some sign of an auto.

* * * * *

'So when did Anshul propose to you?'

'Uh…h...h, last semester,' Saumya replied, looking stunned at Vineet's acidic tone.

'What did you say?'

'I said yes. I wanted to ask you but...' a feeling of guilt engulfed her.

'That you should have done before accepting his proposal,' he replied, fuming with anger.

Vineet was obviously not in favour of this relationship because of the guy involved.

* * * * *

Shubh's patience had reached its limit. He was completely exhausted with the self-control he had exercised while he was with Avantika so that she wouldn't guess that he treated her more than "just friends", and on the other hand, he also had to face the wrath of his buddies in the hostel because no one liked her.

Some called her plastic, others a good actress; some called her a sycophant and a few others called her selfish. There were many names by which she was addressed but Shubh was indifferent to it all. For him the only face which could bring a smile on his face was hers. Her one look could make his day. His sense of direction in life was set by Avantika's presence. He cried for her and he fought against everyone's objection of her.

Nearly everybody in college knew about his obsession except for the person who ought to have known before anybody else. But Shubh was plagued by one fear and that prevented him from taking any step.

* * * * *

The bond between Saumya, Meenakshi, Deepti and Saniya grew stronger day by day. Saniya was the most flamboyant of all in the sense that she was the most frank among them all. Her ear-splitting laughter and openness even stumped me in the beginning.

We had many things in common, like a similar feeling of contempt for books. She was unaware of the word "stress" and if she did feel it, then it was only in the company of her moron friends.

'Saniya, are you free?' I asked.

'Yeah, I mean sort of, but why?'

'This "principle of programming languages" is extremely boring, so I thought we could help each other in completing it.'

'It's true *yaar*, this stuff is bloody crap,' Saniya affirmed. I imagined a cigarette dangling from her fingers while speaking to me, 'So what is on your mind?'

I came back to the reality with a jolt. 'Oh, I was saying that if we read two pages each and explained each other the gist, then it would be easier and far less tedious.'

‘That sounds like a good idea,’ she remarked. I looked at Saumya who was sitting on a bench just behind ours. She was all ears at our conversation instead of minding her business. ‘But what about Saumya?’

‘What about her? *Arrey* she won’t mind. She was the one who proposed that we both should study separately during the sectionals so that we wouldn’t disturb each other,’ I replied, looking at Saumya from the corner of my eye. Her face was distorted with anger. I grinned mischievously.

‘Are you sure?’

‘One hundred and one per cent; we give each other so much space that sometimes I feel that I am on earth and she in space.’

‘Okay, so let’s start. We have a lot of ground to cover, ma’am.’ *Dude, I was still okay in flirting.*

So that was the start of a lifelong partnership between two wandering souls.

14

Knock Out

The best thing about third year in college was that we were to be allocated a single room. I was exploring a range of new dimensions and for that I needed privacy. Everyone was more or less happy with this arrangement except for Aayush, for whom a group was synonymous with his identity and this new arrangement robbed him of his identity. Vineet was used to living in chaos. Aayush and I shared the same lobby, while the rest of them were in the adjacent one.

* * * * *

With the third year in the reckoning, a new war was about to start. The race to presidency of the only activity club of our jail, known as *Yuva*, had begun. The change of guard was about to commence at the end of the fifth semester. The presidency was open to boys and girls alternately and this year the president had to be a girl. The catfight had already begun. On one side was Avantika, the topper in CS, the most sophisticated and diplomatic girl, while on the other side was the college topper at that time and a top model, a perfect combination of beauty and brains, Hrishita.

Both of them didn't see eye to eye right from the beginning of the college. Hrishita was the obvious preference for our nymphomaniac MD due to his sweet tooth for good-looking females. Avantika had some strong backing of the Dean who was a family friend belonging to the same caste. It might sound ridiculous but castes did play a major role in the battle for power. Apart from him, another person who was a big cheerleader for Avantika was the outgoing president, Sandeep, who harboured a soft corner for her.

In this power tussle, Shubh again took a back seat as Avantika was now very busy with her campaigning or spent most her time either with her favourite Sandeep or at the *Yuva's* small office, attending to some paper work. Bureaucracy at every stage can be highly ineffective and one could understand the working of the entire Indian officialdom by seeing the specimen in that small office where decisions were taken merely to pass time and then forget them as soon as office closed down.

Shubh knew that if Avantika were to become the president, then his every possible chance of being with her would be ruined but nevertheless, he wanted her to win because she was desperate to get it.

The more Shubh drifted towards Avantika, the more he wafted away from everyone else. His childhood friendship with Pawan was nearly over. Pawan's downhill journey was racing fast without any halt. He lost face when he got a black paper in his fourth semester while Shubh climbed the ladder of academic success at an equal speed.

* * * * *

Pawan never showed he needed support from anyone but now he really wanted somebody to lift him up. He knew that his best friend was no longer with him. The rift between them was increasing with every passing day. Pawan's loneliness was killing him every day and that only increased the intake of his cigarettes. He however found, solace in the company of Kunal.

Kunal was one of the good students in CS-1 as well as decently good looking. He was tall, fair complexioned than most of the girls in the college and was blessed with sharp features. The only thing that was an eyesore about him was his girl-like demeanour which put off everyone who came in contact with him. Kunal and Pawan hit it off instantly because Kunal too felt like the odd guy out and their exact opposite natures facilitated an instant rapport. Kunal didn't like the way hostlers lived and behaved and as the proximity between the two grew, Pawan became more and more distant with everyone else.

* * * * *

Undoubtedly some were drifting apart, but there were some souls who were drawing nearer to each other.

'Someone is studying hard,' Vineet snorted.

'Oh, someone is talking to me,' Deepti replied.

'So where is everyone else or did they ditch you? I already suspected this and that's why I warned you to control your tantrums and anger.'

'Sorry to disappoint you, but I wanted to be alone and look who is talking about anger management.'

'How much time has passed since we talked to each other the last time?'

'I don't know; may be a few months.'

'It is more than a year, to be precise.'

'Really, I never felt it.'

'And about anger management, according to my sun sign, it suits me. I am a Leo, you know.'

'And so is mine.'

'So how come you are alone?'

'Stop being so smart with me.'

'But people do need an explanation.'

'Oh is that so? Then make one for your sake.'

'I thought we were never going to talk again.'

'Same here but I don't want to carry on with silly fights and petty arguments.'

'You remember the reason why we were not talking to each other? I don't remember it.'

'I told you it was petty.'

'So we are friends again?'

'Okay.' A big toothy smile came on Vineet's face.

* * * * *

'What happened? Why are you fuming like this?' Aayush asked.

'Nothing *yaar*, this Rajiv is really a pain in the ass.'

'That I know but what did he do this time?' Aayush asked, smiling widely.

'*Arrey yaar*, since the morning he has been pestering me by accompanying me to the college, sitting down with me, sharing lunch with Avantika and Mandakini and escorting me even when I wanted to see off Avantika. What is most irritating is that he sleeps on my bed, uses my towel and if I talk to someone, he wants to know who it is that I talked to and why the other person called. If I want to go to the canteen, he instinctively begins to feel famished. Gawd, he really is getting on my nerves. At least my shadow is better than him as it leaves me when the lights are called off,' Shubh kept on ranting.

'I didn't know that he was such a jerk.'

'Now I can't even hope to spend a few minutes with Avantika.'

'Why don't you tell this to his face?'

'I don't want to hurt him. I am the only guy who talks to him and if...'

'Then keep facing what you are already facing.'

'I think you are right. I will tell him right away that he is making my life one bloody hell.'

'That's my boy, all the best.'

'Thanks Aayush,' and Shubh left.

* * * * *

'Do you know what happened in the morning?' asked Aayush and began to describe his conversation with Shubh.

'What do you think? Will he be able to speak out his mind?' I asked.

'Yeah, why not?'

'It's good if he can, though I am afraid he will not be able to do it.'

'And why do you think so?'

'For the simplest reason that firstly, Rajiv is the only guy who supports him in his pursuit of Avantika and secondly, Shubh needs someone who can support him without becoming a contender and Shubh's social life is in a mess due to his involvement with Avantika. Many of his social acquaintances are now making fun of him and criticising him openly when, for Shubh, it is very important to know what others think about him. He is averse to criticism of any sort. He wants Rajiv ever more desperately.'

'I don't think so. Shubh has been rather put off with Rajiv of late.'

'You wan'na bet on this?'

'Okay, dinner in canteen from whoever loses.'

'You have money or not?'

'Shut up,' and we laughed out aloud.

But Shubh, as usual, failed again and I won the bet.

* * * * *

'Did you check the notice-board?' Aayush asked.

'No. Why?' I was in the class with Saumya. Meenakshi was seated at the back with Saniya and Deepti.

'HP is conducting campus recruitment in Moradabad for our batch.'

'What? When? What's the criterion?' I found myself getting energised after a very long time.

* * * * *

Everybody was excited about their first campus interview.

'Should I talk to Meenakshi to convince your family?'

'Anshul, it's not my family, but Papa who is against my taking up any kind of job.'

'So, should I talk to him?'

'No, and I mean a big NO.'

'Then at least ask him once.'

'He won't agree. He won't let me go outside Bareilly.'

'Then why the heck is he wasting money on your

education here? If he wanted you to be a graduate only, then why didn't he send you for a B.Sc. degree and the same goes for your sister?'

'I don't know,' Saumya said nonchalantly.

'Then please do me the favour of asking him,' I found myself getting angry at Saumya for her indifference.

* * * * *

Aayush and I were waiting in his room for everyone to get ready. Moradabad was at a distance of three hours from Bareilly and we decided to leave a day earlier to be present there well on time.

'Did you ask them to tell us when they intended to leave?'

'Yeah, I told Vineet twice and Shubh once. I think, Anshul, you should buy one mobile phone also.'

'Yeah, I am also thinking the same.'

'How come you don't have a cell phone when you have a girlfriend since the past one year? How come Saumya didn't pester you to buy a cell?'

'I told her that I didn't want to compromise with my privacy when I am in the hostel and she understood.'

'She understood or did you force her to understand? You are such a dog,' Aayush said, looking at my mischievous smile.

'Okay, just check why they are taking so much time?'

After five minutes Aayush returned cursing someone. I picked up my bag and handed his to him. To Aayush's utter surprise, the doors were locked. THEY HAD ALREADY LEFT.

'It happens, *yaar*,' I tried to calm him down.

'No, it doesn't happen. How can it be that not even one of them remembered that we would be waiting for them.'

'I think I saw Vineet in the auto,' I said, pointing at a three-wheeler which raced ahead of us.

'It doesn't matter now.'

We took another auto towards the bus station.

'Where are you guys?' Aayush's phone rang. It was Shubh.

'At the same place where you left us.'

'We left you or you left us?'

'Don't give me crap. We both know who did what?'

'Okay, okay, don't get angry. Just tell me where you are?'

'We are at the bus station.'

'Oh, you have reached there already. We are still in the auto.'

They reached after a few minutes. Shubh wrapped his hand around Aayush in order to do some damage control.

'So how are we going?' Kunal asked.

'By bus, of course. We don't park planes at the bus station,' Rajeev replied sarcastically.

'No, I mean, I travel only by an air-conditioned bus,' Kunal replied hesitatingly.

I looked around, wondering if this was the beginning, what could be the end!

'My uncle has already arranged for a hotel,' Kunal said. Pawan beamed with pride in his eyes.

'One more five hundred rupee note gone into ashes,' Vineet muttered under his breath.

As soon we reached there, we began our search for the hotel to spend a night in. After a little search and negotiation, we settled for a decent but cheap hotel.

'Pawan and I are staying together,' pat came the suggestion from Kunal.

Next morning, a few surprises lay in store for us. The first surprise which we had not even imagined was the number of heads that were visible at the venue. The second and the most cruel surprise was that the written evaluation was meant only for the selected *trainees* for HP and after that, for a training of three to four months, only a handful number of candidates would be selected. The icing on the cake was that the result of the written paper would be declared after a month or so.

Each one of us was hungry, frustrated and angry at that unexpected joke. At the bus stand, we found that the next bus was scheduled to come after three hours.

'So, are we going to wait for three hours in this bloody roasting heat?' I asked, looking at my watch which was stuck at 1 o'clock.

Nobody had the answer. The entire luggage was dumped at the bus station. Aarti was accompanying us when leaving. She and Aayush thought it better to board the next bus as soon it came and it did come soon.

Slowly everyone drifted from the bus station for a smoke or snacks, except for Shubh and me. Thirty minutes and two buses passed, yet there was no sign of anyone. Shubh, who had gone fifteen minutes ago to search for others, did not show his face again. Fifteen more minutes and another bus passed and my temper began to rise. Finally I got up and went outside the bus station to look for them.

'This life sucks, man!' I heard Vineet's voice from a nearby tea-shop.

'You all are eating here while I was waiting there in this heat. At least you could have told me,' I said, looking at

Vineet. 'Three buses have already gone and will anybody tell me how long are we going to stay at this fucking place?'

Vineet glared at me, with a few more eyebrows assisting him and suddenly threw his plate down.

'What happened?' Shubh asked. I was stunned at his reaction.

'I didn't ask you to wait, did I? You can leave at any time you wish. And who are you to tell us what to do and what not? You are just a bloody lecher and I don't take orders from a eunuch.'

'What the hell are you saying?' Shubh shot back.

'Don't stop me, Shubh. Let me tell him his real worth because nobody else would ever tell him that,' Vineet kept on talking like a drunkard. 'Well Mr Anshul, we all hate you because you are so very selfish. You don't simply fit in with us because you don't have the courage to face the truth and the truth is that we have always detested you. And today we are leaving you here because you are not worth sitting with us,' Vineet said, standing up. Vijay joined him.

He looked at Shubh who remained rooted to his place. Then he again glared at me as if accusing me of robbing his best friend from him and left.

I was shell-shocked. I felt as though a thousand needles had been pierced in my head in a minute. I was filled with emotions. Vineet and Vijay had gone but left me with an experience of a lifetime. I didn't look at anybody; I simply just couldn't.

When I reached the bus station, a bus drove past me. Vineet and Vijay's bag were missing. We boarded the next bus.

'That was not good.'

'Yeah, that should not have happened.'

Everyone was voicing his opinion, but I was least interested in any of that. My mind was still replaying what all had just happened. We reached the hostel around seven. I had my dinner and retired to my room for the much needed sleep.

* * * * *

'WHAM...WHAM...BH…A….A…M!' *Was I dreaming?* 'BHAM...WHAM!' The thrashing kept on unrelentlessly.

'Who is it?' I shouted sleepily.

Nobody responded but the hammering went on like a never-ending noise.

I stood up, mustering up all my energy and thinking that it could be Aayush.

A hand grabbed my neck as soon as I opened the door. 'You are trying to turn my friends against me.'

'Vineet, what the hell are you doing?'

'What do you think you are. A hero? A martyr? And I am a loser? I will show you who is the hero here.'

'Vineet, if you want to talk, we can do so.' But his grip tightened on my neck. He punched me on my skull twice.

'Leave him, Vineet,' came Aayush's voice as he opened the door and grabbed Vineet from behind.

A few more joined him and took Vineet back to his room. I sat down on the floor, still reeling with the sudden attack and shock.

'Stand up Anshul and come inside. Sit down over here.' Aayush helped me to sit down on his bed. Tears rolled down my cheeks. Something inside me had broken and I could not place my finger on it. Everything had come to an end, everything.

* * * * *

Saumya questioned me a number of times on what had happened in Moradabad, but I didn't want to tell her anything as all I wanted to do was to forget it. Many things had been changed after that night.

* * * * *

The sixth semester started with a bang. A new company had shortlisted our college for campus placement which was to take place in Ghaziabad. The criteria dampened the spirits of many. Not everyone was happy about the terms and conditions, particularly the essential qualification of having scored seventy per cent marks in every semester with no backlogs. In any case, all of us reached there to try out our luck.

Many of the confident toppers were left high and dry in the written paper itself. Shubh, Avantika, Kunal, I and many others were asked to leave the campus through a small notice displaying the names of the selected aspirants. It was an eyeopener for many of us because out of some four thousand aspirants, only twenty-one were selected for the next round and subsequently, out of twenty-one, only seven were finally selected. And among those seven, only two were from our college – Meenakshi and Deepti.

And thus began the race in which no one wanted to be left behind. Soon everyone became busy with something or anything that would even remotely assure him or her a place in a good company with a decent package. The next company that everyone was eager to get in was about to come for selection of candidates in April. Barely three weeks were left and everyone seemd cocooned in his own world with no time for anyone else.

This alone was not the important preoccupation for everyone. The other was the selection of the new president for the *Yuva* club. Both Avantika and Hrishita had geared themselves up for the final round.

Finally the day came when a small notice with a much smaller font intimated us that Avantika headed the list which contained a few surprises. Soon the list of various office-bearers was put up on the notice-board. Shubh became the vice-chairman, sports; Vijay, the vice-chairman, literary activities; Shubh grabbed the opportunity to stay with Avantika with all of his thirty-two teeth never stopping to grin. Now his time was only for Avantika.

15

The Kiss

Excitement was in the air. The atmosphere became rather tense but it was expected.

My life had now become very steady with no time for gossip or bitching about anyone, which was a part and parcel of the group in which I was previously involved. I had only two time slots left in my life – one was reserved for Saumya and the other to devote to my own life in which I read books, listened to music and watched movies apart from hanging with Aayush while we played cricket on his computer.

I was completely geared for my next outing. I could not afford to lose that opportunity and the one thing that I needed to do was to persuade Saumya to appear in the written test. This was the only company that was visiting our campus and hence that was our only chance to get selected together.

'You are appearing for the written.'

'It's of no use. Even if I get selected, Papa won't send me outside Bareilly.'

'Why won't he send? I want to know the reason.'

'Well, because he loves me and can't imagine seeing me in trouble.'

'Did he tell you all this crap or is it a figment of your imagination?' I said quite rudely.

'Shut up, Anshul.'

'I don't know how a person can be so selfish towards his own child. Just because he can't bear the pain of separation, he will throttle your dreams and aspirations with both his hands just to make his own life comfortable,' I was trembling with rage. Saumya was looking at me astoundingly.

'You don't understand anything,' Saumya said with disgust.

'Then help me to understand; I am all ears. You know, why you can't explain it? It is because you have accepted it as it was presented in front of you. Tell me one thing, do you really want to do the job or is it just another bloom in your fairyland?'

'You know that I really want to be with you and for that I will do anything.'

'Don't give me crap. Just answer my question.'

'Yes, I want to do the job if it is the only way to be with you.'

'Then let me make you aware about some of the facts.'

'Then tell me, had you been in my place, what would you have done?'

'First of all, I would never have sat idle with my hands folded and I would have tried to convince Uncle by first convincing Aunty and Udita. Then I would have used the most dangerous weapon for all of mankind.'

'What's that?'

'First promise me you won't tell anyone about the warhead.'

'Anshul, don't irritate me *naa.*'

'It's your tears,' I whispered, clearly afraid of being overheard.

'You are nuts.'

'Try it before calling me a trickster.'

'I won't need them. I am appearing in the written test.'

'That's my baby elephant.'

'Um…m…m…m *Maar doongi.*'

* * * * *

That day tension and anxiety were at their height. The written was scheduled for 2 o'clock in the afternoon. Aayush, Saumya and I were placed in the same batch. Time seemed to be flying like an eagle, eager to grip me with my neck.

Sitting in that large hall, I was sweating like a stinking pig. I only remember the moment when a bald, fat man told us to start the online test and then after exact 60 minutes, which seemed to me like 60 seconds, asked us to press the submit button.

The names of the shortlisted candidates were displayed on the notice-board after forty-five minutes that seemed to have been transformed into forty-five years.

'Saumya, you are there in the list,' I announced with excitement.

'And you?' she asked, instead of getting happy.

'I didn't check that. Wait here, I will be right back,' I said amazed at my response.

Everyone was there in the list, right from Aayush to Avantika and Vineet to Shubh.

'WE DID IT!' I heard a victory chant from not so far. I gave a fleeting look in that direction only to find Vineet hugging Shubh, Vijay and Pawan.

A thought crossed my mind about hugging, but Saumya would never allow me to embrace her in public. So I hugged Aayush instead, who was busy with Aarti, celebrating their triumph.

The interviews were scheduled for the next day. I could hardly sleep that day. I felt like my dream was about to be fulfilled.

'Sir, you are next,' a volunteer approached me.

'Yeah okay...thanks,' I fumbled. I checked myself in my reflection on the floor. I looked horrendous. *Gosh, what a disastrous way to begin.* I was busy mentally rehearsing my intro, when a shrill voice broke my thought pattern.

'May I come in,' I attempted to peep through the door. 'Good afternoon, sir.'

'Good afternoon, Anshul.'

That single word put me at ease. *Gosh, he knew my name.* I felt a heavy burden lift off my chest.

After an hour or so and I appeared for the HR round. I saw Saumya going inside the room for this technical round. I tried to smile, but her worried look made me revise my strategy.

'Hi *Anshul,* please have a seat,' a middle-aged man greeted me.

Man I like this company. 'Thank you, sir,' I said, giving the broadest smile possible while sitting down.

It took me sixteen minutes and thirty-five seconds to get out of that room.

Saumya was still inside. I decided to have a quick bite.

'Hey Anshul, how was the interview?' I looked around to locate the speaker.

'It was okay,' I said in a terse voice.

'Mine is about to start,' Vineet said.

'All the best then,' I said, keen to end this small talk.

'Thanks mate,' he smiled forcibly.

I tried to smile but something swirled inside me, which prevented me from doing so.

* * * * *

'How was it?'

'He didn't ask me anything technical, except for two questions,' Saumya said, looking rattled.

'Then what took you so long?'

'He was asking about my hobbies and interests.'

'So what did you answer?'

'I told him that my hobby and passion is food and that too lots of it.'

'So you talked about food and only food for full thirty-five minutes.'

'Yes,' Saumya said, while munching another chocolate.

'Congrats. You are selected for the next round.'

'But he didn't ask me anything technical.'

'Don't worry. Your face has all the answers he could have required.'

'So you want to say that I am pretty,' even the dumbest of the girls could have understood what was meant.

'No, I don't mean anything even remotely like that. I mean he, the interviewer, wanted to say something like that.'

'Um....m....m...! Why can't you say something like... you know.'

'No, I don't know and don't want to know either.'

* * * * *

'Deepti, what happened? Why are you sitting all alone over here? Is anything wrong?' Vineet asked on entering the class.

'I'm alright. Please leave me alone,' Deepti seemed to have been crying as her eyes were moist.

Vineet looked at those trembling lips that were pleading with him to leave, but her large eyes wanted him to stay close. Suddenly somebody whispered in his ears, "*She needs you, you can't go.*"

'Why does this happen with me always? What does he think of himself that he can do whatever he wants...every time. Why does he always break my heart? God, why me? Why did you make me love him?' Tears began to roll down her cheeks.

But Vineet wasn't listening to any of this; nor did he want anyone to come in between. He grabbed Deepti from her shoulders. She looked at him with moist eyes. He wiped her tears. Deepti closed her eyes.

'I love you,' Vineet said softly and kissed her softly on her forehead.

Deepti opened her eyes with bewilderment.

'What are you doing?' Deepti backed off. 'JUST LEAVE,' she screamed.

'I have loved you from the first day that I saw you. No one can love you more than me.'

'Just leave Vineet. Leave me right now.'

Vineet departed with a pinch of salt water visible in his eyes.

* * * * *

'Welcome everyone. It was a rigorous but enthralling experience for us all. I don't know about you guys, I mean, more than two hundred candidates. I mean we were really spellbound at such a large turnout. So give a round of applause to yourself,' the same middle-aged gentleman announced.

The small auditorium resonated with thunderous applause.

'So here are the names of the selected candidates… Aditya (applause), Kruti (more applause)...'

A total of fifty-seven had made it to the finals. ~~Eashaan~~, ~~Aarti~~, Anshul, Avantika, Vijay, Saumya, ~~Vineet~~, ~~Pawan~~, ~~Aayush~~, ~~Saniya~~, and Shubh. Some tears of disappointment and some of elation could be seen in the eyes of those present. No one knew whether to celebrate or to wait till everyone got selected. We decided on the latter.

* * * * *

'Don't worry...you will get a good job.'

'I am not thinking about that.'

'Then?'

'You know what I am talking about,' Vineet said, still avoiding Deepti's eyes.

'Can we avoid talking about that for some time?'

'No, we have to talk about this. If we didn't clear it today, then the day will never come when you will able to sit with me just as you are sitting today. I don't want that. I want it to be the first day of our new bond and I want to tell you clearly that my love for you is immeasurable, but I won't wait for you forever. I am not someone who will live just with a glimmer of hope that we will meet one day and write our own story. It's just not possible for me. I want your answer NOW in yes or no.'

‘But what will others say?’

‘Deepti, just reply YES or NO?’ Vineet looked directly in those large eyes.

‘Vineet, we are so different yet so similar. It won’t work; this relationship won’t work, but still I can’t do anything for the simplest of the reasons that I love you too. I love you more than anyone and even more than you.’

‘What did you say?’ Vineet asked, unable to believe his luck.

‘Nothing,’ Deepti blushed.

‘No seriously, did you just...’

‘’Bye.’

‘Deepti.’

‘Vineet ’bye,’ Deepti said and left with a red face.

* * * * *

Some things are easier said than done.

‘Is it true what I heard just now?’ Eashaan asked, slamming the door of Vineet’s room.

‘Eashaan, just calm down,’ Vineet said, baffled at this sudden outburst which he had expected but not so soon.

‘JUST ANSWER MY QUESTION. IS THAT TRUE?’

‘Yes, it is....’

And then that happened which shouldn’t have happened in any relationship. Vineet’s face bore the mark of five fingers on his face when Eashaan slammed the door on his face.

And that marked the end of everything between them.

16

The Commitment Trivia

Final year in the college arrived with a whimper but hit us on our face with a bang. Gosh...it was the last year of our togetherness (or non-togetherness).

'Who is Udita?' Aayush asked in the class.

'Yes, sir.'

'Come with me.'

'Where, sir?'

'Don't ask stupid questions.'

'But sir, this lecture is not free.'

'So?' Aayush said with a tinge of harshness and left the class.

Udita followed Aayush.

'Oye, where are you taking her?' Saumya asked Aayush on reaching the threshold of the class.

'Didi,' Udita cried.

'It's none of your business,' Aayush snapped.

'Anshul, look Aayush is trying to rag Udita,' she looked at me as Saniya and I drew near them in the corridor.

'So, what can I do?' I said. 'She is your sister, so you should protect her.'

'He is absolutely correct.'

'Saniya, you too,' Saumya complained.

'Off course, me too.'

'Um…m…m….m...! Anshul, stop annoying me.'

'Okay, if she sings a song, then she can leave,' Aayush said.

'Why should she...?' Saumya asked.

'That's easy. I can do that,' Udita interrupted.

Aayush and I looked at her, grinning.

'Which song?' she asked.

'You decide,' I said.

'Okay,' she started with a song but had to stop midway when a faculty arrived.

'Okay, you can go,' I said.

Hence the little sister of Saumya arrived in our lives.

* * * * *

When words remain unspoken, the friction in the heart amplifies. Our brain is a fantastic computer as it records every damn thing we do or which happens to us. Even if we try to forget everything, in our subconscious mind it is always there.

'Hi, how are you?' Vineet said to me, while entering Aayush's room.

I looked at him with a blank expression.

'I said, hi.'

'Hi,' I said.

'Congrats for the job.'

'Thanks,' I said and waited till some awkward moments crawled by.

'So...still angry?'

'About what?'

'You know about what I am talking.'

'I am already over with that.'

'But I am not.'

'Don't worry, it doesn't matter any more. It took me almost two and a half years but finally I know what I want. If it hadn't happened, I would not have known my true worth. I don't need anything from you. It did hurt me a lot at that time but now I know and believe that whatever happens, it happens for good. I can't help you with your problems. You have to solve them for yourself.'

'But I don't know how? What I had done was impulsive and wrong, but now I want to say sorry for everything.'

'I told you, it doesn't matter anymore. If you want to say it, then it's your wish, but I can't give you something that I don't have.'

'But Anshul...'

'Vineet, please don't say anything that might make you and me both....you know what I mean and if you want to say anything to anyone, then the right person is Eashaan.'

'What about Eashaan?'

'I don't know, but you two were bosom pals and now you have allowed everything to fall apart,' I completed.

Vineet chose to keep quiet.

* * * * *

'Hi Eashaan, how are you?'

'How do I look like to you?'

'Why are you so rude? What have I done to you?' Saniya complained in a hurt and tremulous voice.

'Sorry, nothing. I was thinking about something else.'

'About Deepti and Vineet?'

Eashaan remained quiet.

'I know it hurts a lot when you love somebody and the response is far from what you expect,' Saniya said, speaking from her heart. 'But I guess that's what life is all about.'

'I don't know what life is and what it wants from me. I know only one thing and that is, I won't let it happen again to me. I am not going to give anyone the slightest chance to hurt me any more.'

Streets too can be teacher in one's life because they make you stumble and even fall sometimes and get hurt but then, they do teach you a precious lesson.

* * * * *

Rumours about Vineet and Deepti were flying high and large in the college corridor. That single event had changed many equations and strained many hearts. Not only had the friendship between Vineet and Eashaan snapped, but also the relations between Deepti and the other three. Everyone believed that Deepti should not have played with Eashaan's emotions if she had no interest in him.

'Saniya, why are you not talking to me?' Deepti stopped Saniya midway when the latter again tried to escape from Deepti.

'I don't think that I need to tell you that.'

'But I need to know why you are behaving so strangely?'

'You are my best friend but so is Eashaan. And I have seen him suffer since the beginning because of you. I don't think you deserve him but if you have to do this, you should have told him right in the beginning. I know about the messages and texts you used to send him. Tell me, was that all a play or do you enjoy playing with the emotions of others?'

'Saniya, you are crossing your limits.'

'You have already crossed it, so now don't teach me my limits.'

'So what do you want me to do now? Plead for your or his forgiveness?' Deepti screamed.

'No, I don't think you deserve even his forgiveness.'

'How can you say so? How can you forget that just because of him I have had to bear so much.'

'It is nothing compared to what you have done to him.'

'So you want to say that the relationship beween Vineet and me is wrong?'

'You never ever understood, so I am not surprised today. You are talking like the dumbest person I have ever known.'

'Yes, you are right. It is entirely my fault but that's what you think, not me. So I am leaving you both forever.'

'Never ever think that you have left us. It is we who had left you the day you betrayed our trust. I don't have anything else to say. Now, if you will excuse me, I have something important to attend,' said Saniya and left furiously.

Deepti kept looking at the door long after Saniya was gone.

* * * * *

'Anshul, I want to be with you,' Saumya held my hand in hers.

'So, what's the problem? Go ahead and tell your parents.'

'*Kabhi to* serious *raha karo*.'

'So what do you want me to do? You want that I should go and ask your parents to allow us to get married to each other? What if they ask about my profession and how do I expect to keep you happy? Then what do you expect me to say? That I will feed you on love, we will live in the house made of love, sleep on the bed made of love. And then what will you expect them to answer?'

'So do you want to say that we will never get married?'

'MARRIAGE! What are you talking about? Think practically Saumya. How long do you think it will take me to reach a position when I will be able to support a family? Five years, seven years or may be ten years. So will you wait for that long or will your parents allow you to wait for an uncertain happening like that? What are the chances that I will make it to the elite list of professionals in the next five years?'

'So it was all a time pass for you. All guys are same.'

'No it is not so and you know it. Don't get me wrong. I don't want to ruin your life. I don't want you to regret your decision after two years of our marriage or me regretting that I couldn't give you a better life which I could. I really do need time.'

'Time is the only thing that I don't have. I can only give our relationship a maximum of one year and half but after that, I don't know what will happen after that,' Saumya said with finality.

I didn't know what to say because the picture of my parents flashed in my mind who wanted to see me pursuing MBA after my graduation.

* * * * *

'What happened? You are looking worried,' Aayush said, looking at my expression of worry.

I told him about my conversation with Saumya.

'You know what? Aarti too has been pestering me with the same nonsense since the past few weeks. Whenever we meet nowadays, we only fight with each other over this issue. Sometimes I think that all those mushy and romantic moments that we used to spend with each other are a thing of some distant past. Sometimes I really feel sick from all this crap. It would have been better to remain single,' Aayush ranted.

'You are right; these girls have nothing else to do. Their only concern is makeup, bitching about others, creating ruckus on trivial matters and making our lives hell. What do they think life is? Is it so easy to support a family for a young man? All that they have to worry about is what is happening in the other person's house and in their f***ing TV soaps. You only have one year to prove yourself. Are we some kind of scapegoats whose every piece of flesh should be given away?' I joined Aayush.

Commitment is the one thing that every girl wants from her boyfriend and it is the one thing that every man is reluctant to give her. It is a battle of sexes that has been going on for years and will continue doing so for the next many years too.

God please, bless the whole guy-kind.

17

The White Corridor

I was at home waiting for the last semester to kickstart. A feeling of nostalgia overpowered me whenever I thought about my last six months in college. Oh God, only six months were left to endure the whims and fancies of our nymphomaniac chairman and exactly the same number of months were left for me to spend some time with Saumya, Aayush, Saniya and Meenakshi.

* * * * *

'Anshul, pick up the phone.' Mom cried from the kitchen.

I made no attempt to buzz from my place, from watching TV.

'Oh my God, this boy.' Mom finally had to come. She glared at me. I avoided her incessant gaze with the newspaper.

'Hello, Yes Anshul is here. Who is speaking?'

Must be Aayush. I thought.

'Udita!!!! Are you Anshul's classmate?' mom's questions were like a never ending train.

'Udita!!!!!!' I sprang into action. 'Mom, give me the phone.' I literally tried to snatch the receiver. She looked me with a quizzical look but nevertheless gave it to me.

'What will happen to you? Only girls call you. Don't you have any guy as a friend?' Mom left with a swollen face.

'Yeah Udita, what happened? Why are you crying?' I was shocked at her sobbing on the phone.

'Bhaiya, mom and *di* had met with an accident while coming from Nanaji's house today. Both are injured but *di* is very serious.' She kept on crying.

I felt like a knife was cutting through my flesh with every passing moment.

'It can't be true, it is just a nightmare.' I thought. 'It can't be true. This simply can't happen.'

I remained standing near the phone long after the call was over with a hope that someone will tell me that all this was a bad joke or something but nothing happened.

I felt a hand on my shoulder. I turned around to see mom's eyes fixated on me.

'Mom, I had to go. I will explain you everything later. There is a train from Lucknow at 10:30 in the night.'

Tri…n….g….g, trin…g….g…g!

The phone rang bitterly, conveniently crushing my thoughts and bringing me to the present.

It was 3:30 in the morning when I reached Bareilly junction. It wore a deserted look with a few passengers sleeping on the benches and a few on the floor. In the cold winter night, the mild layer of fog seemed to have swallowed up the city. I felt my senses drown in the chilly night.

Half an hour later I was standing in a deserted corridor surrounded with white walls earmarked with red and black spots and a smell that is the trademark of every hospital's corridors. My head reeled under the impact of it all.

'Saumya Arora?' I asked at the reception.

'Room No. 229, second floor.'

I sleepwalked to the second floor and then to Room 229 where ICU was engraved on a metallic plate. I gazed at the metallic plate for an unusually long time when I suddenly felt a soft touch on my elbow. I turned around to find Udita's face with swollen eyes. Saumya's father was standing behind her, looking at me. He seemed tired and exasperated.

'How is Aunty?' I asked.

'She is now fine. Her right hand has been fractured and she received a few injuries on her neck and face,' she said slowly.

'And Saumya?'

Udita broke into tears. I tried to console her but could not.

'Her spinal cord is severely damaged and according to the doctors, her left half of the body has been paralyzed,' Uncle said in a choked voice.

"Paralysis?" I felt as though a streak of lightning had struck me. My senses became numb and I stopped feeling anything.

'I want some sleep,' I heard myself utter when I felt Udita stare at me from some time, may be hoping to get some kind of response.

I found a bench in a lonely corner and lay down on it, with my eyes and senses shut close for the first time in my entire life. Somewhere in my heart I still had the belief that it was my worst nightmare and that when I would wake up, it would all be over.

* * * * *

When I opened my eyes, I found myself in the same white corridor after what it seemed like a long journey of unremitting and whacky dreams. I saw people moving aimlessly here and there, without noticing my presence as though I was invisible or something.

What am I doing here? This was the first question to come to my mind.

'So it was not a nightmare,' I said to myself.

'Yeah it seems not,' I replied back.

'And it is very serious?'I asked.

'Yes it is.'

'What should I do?' I asked another.

'Only the right thing.'

'What are my options?'

'You can just get up and never come back. You can forget all this and all those moments you spent together.'

'And the other option?' I enquired.

'You can choose to stay, you can choose to support her and love her because only you can do everything. She needs you right now more than anything else.'

'So what should I do?'

'You know the answer.'

'Are you sure that I can do it?'

'Yes, I know you can do it.'

'But I don't know what to do?'

'You will get to know of it.'

'Okay, then let's do it.' I felt that my head had never

been so clear.

I got up and washed my face.

* * * * *

'I want to see Aunty,' I told Udita who was sitting at a far corner with Uncle.

She pointed to one door. It was a general ladies' ward. I peeped through the glass pane on the door. A female body lay on the bed with bandages on her right hand and a few covering her face too. A glucose bottle was hung on the side. She was fast asleep.

After getting the assurance that she was fine, I moved from there.

Meeting Saumya was a lot tougher than I had imagined. She was being shifted from the ICU to a private ward when I caught a glimpse of her face. It was badly injured. When I entered her room after an hour or so, she had just woken up and was looking at the window. Her body was surrounded with different kinds of equipment and pipes.

'*Kaisa hai mera betu*?' I said.

She turned her face a little to look at me. She lifted her right hand a little but withdrew to keep it back due to the severe pain that peeped through her eyes.

Tears rolled down her cheeks and she began to sob. The pain in her sorrow kept swirling in my head.

'*Hey bachcha,* what happened? Everything is alright. *Chup ho jao chalo,*' I tried to console her. I looked at her face – she looked so weak and pale. She turned her face to the other side.

'Why did you come here? You should not have. Just leave and never come back. I don't need you,' her voice quivered.

I sat near her bed. Her hand, pierced with needles, lay close to mine. I caressed it softly; it trembled a bit but remained unmoved.

'You know, the doctor has said that you will be on your feet in four weeks. Just four weeks and then we will again sit in the same classroom, just you and me,' I consoled her, giving a meek smile. She was still looking at the window-pane.

'You really want me to go?'

'Yes,' she said without looking at me.

'Okay, I will leave but I want to know why?'

'You know the reason.'

'I don't.'

She kept quiet. Two more tears rolled down her cheeks.

'Do you know the story of Victor?' I interrupted her sobs.

'Who?' she queried.

'Well, in simple words, Victor Frankl was a Jew who was captured and tortured like an animal in the Nazi camps. His whole family was killed in the camps in front of his eyes. The only survivor was his sister. Many of the prisoners went insane and were sent to gas chambers.

'One day when he was alone in his cell, he began to realise the importance of the last freedom of the human will. You know what a human will is, don't you? It is that freedom, which nobody can take away from anybody. It is this which gave him a sense of worth. He decided that no matter what happened to him, it was he alone who could decide the impact of that mishap on himself. He kept the flame burning in his heart until it grew so large that nothing around him could affect him. He became a fountainhead for his fellow prisoners and even for the guards. After he was released from there, he became an inspirational speaker and an example of human will. And you know what? We all have that kind of power, provided we use it. We can't change the circumstances but we can change the outcome.'

She listened with rapt attention.

'And you know what? The doctor has said that you can go home in a month. I hope you are not getting attached to this bed or this room for it will be difficult for you to leave,' I smiled. 'And if you now want me to go, then just order me once and I will whoooooosh, disappear, just like a genie.'

'Did you really ask the doctors?'

'Yes sweety. I did.'

She smiled mildly for the first time.

'Now you take some rest. I will be right back from the hostel after dumping my luggage there. Okay?'

'Okay,' she said softly.

Uncle and Udita were standing outside the room. I glanced at them and patted Udita's hand.

'Everything will be alright,' I wanted to say but couldn't. My throat was choked.

* * * * *

'I want to meet the doctor,' I said after a long pause.

'Come with me,' Uncle said for the first time.

We were soon waiting outside the doctor's room. It was 10:30 in the morning and the crowd of patients was increasing in the corridor. I felt a sense of pity for those who had to come here every day. I mean doctors and nurses.

'Anshul, as I have told Mr Arora about Saumya's spinal cord problem, it has been damaged severely at various places and because of that, her left side of the body is paralysed. We can't do anything until her spine is healed and strong,' the doctor said, sitting on a comfortable chair with the X-ray of Saumya's back.

'How much time will it take to heal completely?'

'I don't know. Normally in these kind of cases, it varies from several months to years.'

'What is the minimum possible time taken by one to recover in this kind of a case?'

'What do you want to ask?' the doctor said fumingly.

'I wanted to say nothing; just wanted to know a few things,' I said.

'We don't have this kind of information as it is like one in a million case.'

'Okay, thanks for your time, doctor.' It was time to leave.

* * * * *

'Uncle, tomorrow the registration for the next semester begins. If Udita submits Saumya's registration form, it will be terrific,' I said.

'See Anshul...it is nice that you came here in this condition but now your work here is over. I request you to please leave Saumya and us to our own fate,' Uncle said in a pleading voice.

'Uncle please, I need a little faith from your side on me. There is no harm in the registration; if she gets fit then she will be able to complete her graduation. And about my work, it is just started. I hope you will understand me,' I said, hiding my shock at his abrupt attitude.

* * * * *

For me the college now had no importance in my life. The most precious gift of my life was suffering in the hospital and what was I doing? Only talking. As soon as the college reopened, people started coming to me with words of sympathy and sometimes, pity.

'What happened? How is Saumya? Don't worry, she will be alright.' I felt how shallow some words become when uttered by certain people. Some felt relieved that my perfect life now had something that I could mourn about and at which they could feel elated. Life is lonely if you are in a mess. Meenakshi and Saniya, both came together to see Saumya and Aunty but with instructions to behave as though everything would be fine within a few days. And this time Meenakshi didn't argue with me. I thanked God for small mercies.

Saumya had lost all hope in life and that also included her cute smile which never failed to sweep me off my feet whenever I saw her.

* * * * *

'Hi *musi musi haasi*,' I greeted Saumya. 'What are you doing?'

'Nothing, just snoozing in this goddamn bed all day,' she said in a frustrated tone.

'Okay, I have a surprise for you,' I said in the same chirpy voice.

'I don't want any surprises. God has given me enough.'

'Okay, if you don't want it, at least you can take a look at it.'

'What is it...a scrapbook?'

'And I want you to write something on this, for me.'

'Anshul, I am very tired and I don't think I can write anything.'

'Okay fine,' I snapped.

'Don't get angry. Okay, tell what is it that you want me to write?' she said, looking at my face.

'First, we will adjust your bed. Here is the pen and here is the book. Just try to hold it gently; very well. Now we are ready.'

'Okay, tell me.'

'Well, first can I get a smile?'

'Anshul, don't start it all over again.'

'Okay, okay, if you don't want to give me anything, it's fine but at least you can take this from me.'

A small smile came on her face after looking at the rose bud in my hand.

'Okay, okay, now we are going to write something,' I rubbed my palms. 'First we will write the date, that is 1st of March.'

'But this is next month's date.'

'Yes, it is, but it will be better if you don't ask stupid questions.'

She wrote it, though painfully.

'I, Saumya Arora, am happy to be back on my feet on this bright sunny day...don't look at me, just write... without any support and on you own. Completed? Good.'

'Anshul, it would be better if you stop behaving like a kid. You can't imagine how difficult it is for me, just to breathe and face life every day. I don't know why he has left me alive? It would have been a lot better if I had died. And do you think this is some kind of a movie where everything gets okay in the end? Unfortunately, it is not. Please, I beg of you, forgive me and if possible, forget me. We can't be together; we don't have any future and stop coming here because you feel pity for me. If you have ever loved me, then please don't come here again,' she said, tears rolling down her eyes.

I quietly stood up and dashed out of the room.

* * * * *

An hour or so had passed.

'So where is everyone?' I asked.

'I thought you went to the hostel!' Saumya exclaimed.

'I too thought about it but then I felt very hungry, so I thought it better to eat something before going anywhere,' I said, patting my stomach.

'Papa has gone home to bring dinner and Udita is sleeping in Mom's ward.'

'Wow, so we are alone in this large room? Cool.'

'Anshul, what do you want?'

'Wow *yaar*, I didn't knew that you were so fast. I didn't expect such a direct question from you,' I said, rolling my eyes.

'Anshul!!'

'Okay, okay, actually I want to ask one very simple question. Will you marry me?'

'Anshul, stop kidding me.'

'I am not kidding you; I just want to know one thing. That is....okay, okay don't cry now...okay, I am going, I am going.'

'I love you,' Saumya was sobbing.

'Oh…h…h…h... my *betu,* I love you too.'

I held her hand—it was soft like always.

'So the first thing I want is that you won't cry any more.'

'I will,' she said.

'Sorry.'

'I will marry you.'

'Thank you, my royal highness.'

'What do you want me to do? I will do whatever you will ask me to do,' she said with a great show of vigour.

'Okay, the second thing I want is that you will start believing every word I tell you to write in this scrapbook.'

'I believe you.'

'Just promise that you will never behave like a pessimist, that you will never lose hope and will fight for your share of happiness.'

'I promise.'

'That's my girl. Get ready to roll my dear; we have a deadline to meet.'

And so a race began against time. Sometimes we need to fight for our share of life and I couldn't afford to lose Saumya.

18

The Acid Test

Meanwhile my college continued at a steady pace. Everyone was busy with plans for their future. The latest fad was of falling in love if the two from the opposite sex were in the same company. And those who were not in the same company, like Aayush and Aarti, well, Aayush's Mom had clearly voiced her view that Aarti was not cut out for the role of their daughter-in-law. Aarti clearly didn't like the judgement and asked Aayush to either convince his Mom or break up with her.

Meenakshi and Saniya still sat together in class while Deepti now sat with someone else. On the other hand, Saniya was confident that Saumya would make it after hearing that her registration had been done by her uncle.

Eashaan and Saniya now spent most of their time together in college. What Saumya had to face once was now being faced by Saniya – that is, balancing her time in college between Eashaan and Meenakshi.

Saniya told me that Eashaan had proposed to her but she was still in a dilemma about what to reply to him.

'Hey, Anshul are you free?'

'Yeah, tell me.'

'I don't know whether I should ask this at this time or not? I know you are already under great stress.'

'Okay then, do not tell me. If you think you want to be formal with me despite knowing me so well, it's better for you to keep it to yourself.'

'No, Anshul, actually a few days back Eashaan had proposed to me.'

'Okay, that's good news. So what's the problem?'

'The problem is that I don't know what to say to him.'

'So are you thinking that if you say yes, then you might be hurting Deepti in the process and if you say no, then you will definitely be hurting yourself?'

'Yeah, I think so.'

'Do you like him? I mean, as more than a friend.'

'I guess so.'

'Don't guess, be clear about it. Once you are clear in your head, then you won't have to ask anybody what to do or what not to do. And about Deepti, I think she has chosen her path, so she won't mind.'

'I don't know.'

'Don't worry, take your own time. Everything will be sorted out.'

'May be you are right.'

* * * * *

Avantika and Shubh were now mostly missing from the college as most of their time was spent in the newly built office of the *Yuva* club with each other.

Pawan and Kunal were seen in each other's company and all this made Vineet more and more edgy. He did not like everyone being so self-engrossed. Aayush and Aarti continued having araguments over the remarks made by his Mom.

Many new things were happening in the college for the first time -- taking the Dean take a decision for the first time on his own about Saumya's exemption from sectional exams.

* * * * *

'Saumya, I want you to repeat this line every day after waking up and before sleeping,' I pointed to the words she had written in the scrapbook. 'And try to visualise yourself walking, playing and running while speaking.'

'Okay,' she agreed, though I could see the signs of hesitancy in her eyes.

Almost two weeks had passed. Saumya's daily task was to read her goal aloud, then write it every two hours while articulating it in front of a small mirror that I had given her for this purpose. Slowly her confidence started growing and she would smile more often, even more than when she was in college. Her belief in her own abilities had started increasing and that was evident in the X-ray, MRI scan and other tests that showed how her spine was recovering and getting stronger with every passing day. Aunty had now started sitting with her most of the time and this really boosted Saumya's self-confidence.

With just four weeks left for 1st March to begin, I asked Saumya, 'What is your deepest fear?'

'What kind of question is this?' Saumya asked in reponse, looking aghast.

'What is your biggest fear?'

'Losing you,' she said without blinking an eye.

'Well, the news is that I don't believe you.'

'What can I do to make you believe me?'

'A very simple thing – just place your left hand on my hand.'

'Anshul, what are you saying? You know that...'

'I don't know anything except this that either you'll do this or it would be better for us to forget each other,' I said, getting annoyed.

'Anshul, stop playing such games and I don't like such jokes either.'

'You like me to sit beside you the whole day while you keep staring at that stupid fly like a dumbo. Listen, I have had enough of this bullshit. I can't sit here all my life watching you; I have my life also to take care of. And it would be better if we decide right now whether our relationship is feasible or not.'

'Anshul, please don't say this. I will die without you.'

'Then it would be better for you to die. In any case, you wanted to be dead rather than alive, so be it.'

'Anshul, I love you, I really do. Please don't say all these things.'

'Then prove it. Put your left hand on mine.'

'Bhaiya, what are you saying?' Udita interrupted.

'Shut up, Udita, it's between her and me. Prove it Saumya that you love me.'

'Stop it *bhaiya*, you are torturing her,' Udita bellowed.

I could see the tension rise on Saumya's face – her eyebrows frowned, her eyes became moist and drops of sweat covered her forehead, her body shivered due to anxiety while her eyeballs were fixed on me.

'Di, please stop it.'

'Leave it; you don't love me,' I said mockingly.

Her veins bubbled with blood due to which her white skin became red. Her hand remained unmoved.

'Udita, what happened? Why are you shouting?' Aunty and Uncle came inside the room on hearing Udita's cry.

Udita held Saumya's shoulder and Saumya's grip loosened after seeing her mother's face. She was sweating profusely in the air-conditioned room. I got up slowly and went outside. At the door, I turned back to catch a glimpse of Saumya's face. She was crying. I smiled and left.

'Are you insane?' Uncle roared.

'What the hell do you think of yourself? Are you some kind of a hero or what? Do you know how damaging it can be for her recovery?' reprimanded the doctor.

I was sitting in the doctor's chamber with four pairs of squinting eyes trying to cut through my skin.

'I advise you, Mr Arora that for Saumya's well-being it's better if this gentleman is prohibited from talking to her,' the doctor continued.

'Why?' I asked.

'Why? Are you asking me the reason?' the doctor said with anger.

'Yeah, I want to know the reason,' I said.

'Okay, then listen. She is right now very fragile, both physically and mentally. Her spine is recovering but the kind of shock you gave her yesterday can send her back to her previous state. Now do you understand?'

'Last time I told you not to meet her any more for your good, but this time I don't want you to meet my daughter ever for her sake,' Uncle screeched.

'How much do you love your daughter?'

'What kind of crap is this?'

'Did you adopt her?'

'Watch your words, boy. You are crossing your limits.'

'Then why can't you see that she is going to walk, run and play like before as I do?'

'*Ladke*, I warn you not to meet her again,' said Uncle and prepared to leave the room in exasperation.

'I don't think I am going to follow your advice.'

'I'm her father.'

'I never doubted that, but I want to hear directly from her that she does not want to see me.'

'There is no need. My decision is final.'

'Unfortunately, it's not. I want hers.'

'OKAY, I WILL ASK HER,' Aunty interrupted tersely.

'Thank you, Aunty but in front of me only.'

'Okay,' Aunty agreed.

* * * * *

'Hi Saumya, how are you?' I said on entering the room.

'Hi,' a weak smile appeared on her face.

'I came to say goodbye forever,' I said.

'What?' Saumya along with everyone exclaimed!

'Yeah, you know after yesterday's event, I felt that you don't reciprocate my feelings. So it's better if we part our ways now, rather than later when it would be a lot more painful. This decision was very difficult for me but you know now it had to be taken some day. May be I was not able enough to invoke the same feelings in you as I have had for you and it was really my fault. So, I am standing in front of you to seek leave from you. I hope we will meet soon in college, though as friends.'

Everyone was staring at me in amazement at my unexpected U-turn.

'Thank you all, for allowing me to spend some quality time with Saumya,' I said looking at Aunty, Udita and Uncle.

Saumya looked stunned and all blood seemed to have drained from her face. I turned around to pick my belongings lying on the chair and as I was about to leave, I turned to look at Saumya for the last time.

''Bye,' I said softly and left the room.

With every step I felt I that carried a heavy load on my feet. My heart was wrenched with the fear of never seeing her again. I battled with my heart which told me to go back to her. *What was I doing?*

'*Bhaiya, Bhaiya*,' I heard Udita's voice from behind as I waited for the lift. Tears were flowing down her eyes.

'What happened?' I asked.

'Saumya di...come with me.'

I started running behind her.

'Oh God…' I began to pray fervently, hoping for the best.

On reaching her room, I saw Saumya's left hand up in the air, waiting for my hand to rest upon. I quickly reached the edge of the bed and held her left hand as delicately as I could. Tears poured from everyone's eyes except that of the doctor and me. I looked at him with a smile in my eyes. He nodded his head in agreement and smiled in return.

Everyone began to cheer and clap. She had proved that she loved me more than I did.

'I love you,' I said affectionately.

She closed her eyes with tears rolling down her cheeks.

Folks, it was party time.

* * * * *

With three more weeks to go, another incident took place that made us the favourite couple in the corridors of the hospital. Everyone in the college soon came to know about this incident and with some *masala* added, it became a lighting torch for many of the Romeos and Juliets of our love-deprived college.

'Hello Udita, you are Saumya's sister, right?' the Dean asked Udita while she was going to the canteen.

'Yes sir.'

'How is Saumya?'

'She is fine, sir.'

'I have heard some rumours, so I thought I should ask you how far it is all true?'

'Sir, as I don't know what you have heard, how can I comment on them?'

'Oh yes, you are right. Okay you can go,' the Dean replied, looking rather disappointed.

* * * * *

Questions were many but the answers were few. But one question that bogged everyone was what could have happened to Anshul? Was he really in love with Saumya? I myself could not say with certainty. Was I in love? Then why was it that I didn't feel the way they showed in movies or wrote in novels? I really didn't know the answer. But one thing I knew was that my task was still not over. Our dream was still like an unfinished symphony. I needed some kind of motivation to make Saumya stand on her feet and I found the reason soon enough.

* * * * *

'Hey look, what I got for you?' I said excitedly on entering the room.

'What?'

Everyone present in the room looked at me and hence comfortably crushed all my hopes of kissing Saumya.

'Well, we have got the offer letter. Finally we will be joining the company of our dreams.'

Everyone's face which was lighted a while ago now turned into a fused bulb except for Saumya's, as she seemed confused at her state of happiness.

'What? Isn't that great?' I asked.

'*Beta*, we don't think Saumya would be interested in doing a job outside Bareilly.'

'But Aunty, this is a great chance that people would give anything to get and I really think she should not miss this one.'

'Anshul, I know you have done a lot for her and for us also, but I don't want her to do anything outside this city. She can do whatever job she wants in Bareilly but she can't go out of this city.'

'Uncle, but nothing is here. This city is akin to a village and what are you talking about? If she can earn twenty-five thousand, then why do you want her to be satisfied with only a measly salary of eight or nine thousand? And she is also interested in...'

'Anshul, she is not going anywhere and that's final,' Uncle said firmly.

How easily the parents could kill the ambitions and aspirations of their children under the cover of being their child's well-wishers. Bullshit!

'Anshul, I really want to do this job. I don't want to be stuck in Bareilly forever. I'd like to go outside. I want to travel and I want to feel free and fly high in the sky,' Saumya said to me when Uncle left for dinner.

'Don't worry, you will do the job. Just do as I say, okay?'

'Okay.'

'You know what? Your father is a real headache. I have never met a stubborn person like him. I don't know what would happen if we were to get married.'

'Shut up, Anshul. I will kill you if you say anything against him.'

'Really?'

'Really,' Saumya laughed.

Ten days left for 1st March and Saumya started doing chiropractic exercises for strengthening her spine and nervous system. The doctors, who were pleased at her healing, were now all the more happier to see the speed at which Saumya seemed to be on the road to recovery. Saumya had started feeling a tinkling sensation in her feet and it seemed that days of her full recovery were not far.

'Hello Saumya,' Saniya and Meenakshi greeted in unison.

'Hi, Saumya,' Aayush followed behind along with Shubh, Mandakini, Avantika, Vineet and Eashaan.

'Hi,' Saumya beamed.

'Wait, somebody else is also here,' Shubh said.

Saumya looked anxiously at the door. The whole computer science class stood outside the room to meet her.

'Oh…h….h…h, thank you all for coming.'

'How are you?' Avantika enquired.

'I am better than before. How is college going on?' Saumya responded.

'Not good without you,' Eashaan said.

'Well I am coming back soon.'

'Hey, where is Anshul?' Meenakshi asked.

'Why? You want to fight with him?' Vineet asked.

'I am not an arsonist like you,' Meenakshi replied.

Saumya felt a tinge of happiness on seeing that at least for her sake, some differences had been put aside.

'Everyone here knows who is what.'

'Stop it guys, at least in the hospital. Anshul, I think, has gone back to the hostel. He left a few minutes before you all came.'

'Not to worry; we will catch him in the hostel,' Aayush said. 'Anyways, this is for you from all of us,' he said, handing her a larger-than-life teddy bear.

'Oh…h…h…h, it's so cute. Thank you.'

'Okay let's go outside and let others come and meet Saumya,' Avantika suggested.

'Sometimes geeks also speak sense. Okay 'bye Saumya,' Vineet said.

''Bye everyone and thanks again for coming,' Saumya beamed.

'Bye, we will come again,' Shubh said.

'Don't worry, I am soon joining you all guys.' Saumya's confidence took everyone by surprise.

* * * * *

'Anshul, look what I have got? A teddy bear. Isn't it a cutesy pie? *Hai na?*'

'Well, it is, but it is not as cute as you are,' I said, planting a kiss on Saumya's forehead.

'Hey, what is in your bag?' Saumya said looking at my bag.

'Nothing,' I said, hiding it from her.

'Show me, show me. I want to see,' Saumya entreated.

'Okay okay, wait.' I took out a white polybag from my shoulder bag. 'This is for you.'

'SAREE! For me?' Saumya exclaimed!

'Mom and Papa are coming to Bareilly,' I broke the news.

'WHAT? WHEN? WHY DIDN'T YOU TELL ME EARLIER?' Saumya was almost screaming.

'I got the news today itself and for God's sake, stop behaving like one possessed.'

'They are coming here, to Bareilly?'

'Yeah, that's what they have said and they might come here to meet you.'

'Here, in the hospital? Oh my God, I can't meet them in this condition. Look at me Anshul, I am a disaster right now. Look at my face; it is filled with pimples and acne. I can't meet them with this face.'

I felt a flow of mirth at her response. Even in her not-so-good condition, her only concern was her looks. Girls are really the strangest creatures of God!

'I want you to wear this saree when they come to meet you,' I said.

'What are you saying? How can I...?'

'Look Saumya, I want you to look the most stunning girl on this universe when my parents meet you. You are close to your recuperation. Just keep doing what you are doing and everything will be fine. Remember, I am always there with you.'

'Huh.'

'They might arrive here next week.'

'But Anshul, the time at my disposal is so little. How can I?'

'Trust me and have a little faith in yourself. And one more thing, do not tell this to your parents. Okay?'

* * * * *

'*Triveni Express*' reached the Bareilly junction. I touched the feet of my Mom and Papa.

'How are you, my kiddo?' Mom asked.

'I am good.'

'Don't lie to me. Just look at yourself and why have you not shaved? You are looking like a lunatic. Are you stressing yourself too much?'

'No Mom, just forgot to shave. So where are you going to stay?' I asked, looking at Papa.

'Near Izzatangar where one of my friend lives. Do you know where it is?'

'Yeah, I know. It's on the way to my college.'

'Look at your hair. Why are they so long? You are not taking care of yourself. You are looking so weak,' Mom continued.

'Mom, hostellers are like me only. Don't expect us to be like Dara Singh or something.'

'Don't give me nonsensical reasons. It's because of that girl, I know. What's her name?'

'Mom, can we talk about it later and it is not because of her or anyone else.'

'I know everything. Don't tell me.'

'Can we go?' I asked.

It took us one hour to reach their friend's house.

'Okay Mom, I am going to my college. I will meet you in the evening.'

'Okay.'

* * * * *

The most talked about character in this world is the mother-in-law. Many conspiracy theories have been written, several plots have been hatched and numerous attempts have been made to eliminate this character from the soil of this planet but to no avail. Without this character, nothing can be started and once started, nothing can be stopped.

The first meeting between Mom and Saumya was about to occur though not in the manner I had visualised. My mind had stopped working as time passed by. The clock seemed to be running at double speed.

Since the past few days Saumya had become more than eager to stand on her feet. She was working with all her passion and energy to be fit before the doomsday. I mean the day when she would meet my Mom. Her efforts were painful and the doctor had advised her to take it easy and not overstrain herself.

We reached the hospital in the afternoon and headed straight to her room. Everything was happening at a breakneck speed. As I neared the room, I felt my ears drumming or did I hear a noise coming out from the room? I couldn't tell the difference. As I reached closer, it became clear that the noise was emanating from the room.

Inside I saw Uncle, Aunty, Udita, Meenakshi, Aayush, Saniya, Shubh, Vineet, Eashaan and a few nurses along with the doctor standing in a semi-circle and applauding Saumya as she stood in the middle of the room. She looked at me and with her hands stretched and a beaming smile on her glowing face, she walked towards me. She was taking small steps with great difficulty but she was ultimately *WALKING*. I looked at her with astonishment. She inched closer to me and finally rested her hands on my shoulders. We both stood facing each other, looking into each other's eyes while conveniently forgetting that everyone in the room was looking at us. That was the best moment of my life; no, our lives.

'Saumya, this is my mother and my father,' I returned to the earth.

'*Namaste* Uncle, *namaste* Aunty,' Saumya reddened on sensing their presence.

* * * * *

I looked at Saumya; she was sitting on the bed, chatting animatedly with Meenakshi and Saniya. I excused myself and left the room. The corridor was almost deserted. Everything that I had always detested about hospitals now looked so good to me. Drops of tears rolled out from my eyes. Was I crying? But why now, when everything is looking like a marvellous gift of God? No, I was not crying; it was just a delusion.

'*Bhaiya.*' I turned to look behind me. 'Thank you,' Udita whispered.

'Shut up....' I tried to say, but a few more tears rolled down my cheeks. Udita's eyes were also moist.

'*Beta,* she is fine.'

'Yeah, she is fine,' I gave a tight hug to Papa. 'She is fine.'

I just wanted to cry for some time.

I just wanted to savour that moment.

19

The Conspiracy

Saumya's first day in college after recovery made my spirits soar and invigorated me no end. Looking her in the college outfit gave me a sense of longing. I just wanted to cherish the moment when she would begin to laugh and chat with everyone as she did when fit. She looked at me cheerfully; I beamed back.

'Hey, only three months are left,' Meenakshi said.

'I think we should do something to make them memorable,' I replied. After the accident, Meenakshi had changed and had probably realised that I was not that bad as she had thought me to be.

'We are almost bored with these silly little pranks on Aayush. We should change are prey this time. What do you say?'

'Oh my gracious, is Ms. Meenakshi asking me about my opinion?'

'C'mon Anshul, you know that I was never against you.'

'Yeah, yeah! Anyways, forget it. Well, I have an idea but we have to include Saumya also in the plan.'

'What is the plan?'

'Let's wait for Saumya,' I said.

The plan was very simple and according to it we had to make Aayush propose to Saniya, but what seemed tough was how to do it without arousing suspicion.

'I need a love letter from Aayush for Saniya.'

'What? This is impossible. Why would he write a love letter to her?' Saumya asked.

'Nothing is impossible though it could be impossible if you two morons had made the plan without including me,' I said a bit proudly.

'Shut up and tell us what you have in mind,' Saumya patted my cheek.

'Okay, after we will get the love letter, it will be placed in Saniya's bag and then everything will be done automatically.'

'Okay, so the first thing is to write the love letter and that I can do very easily. I only need one of his notebooks,' Meenakshi said excitedly.

'Today is 30th March and we have only two days at our disposal. Saumya, you can do one thing – just implant in Saniya's mind that Aayush feels something more than mere friendship for her.'

'But how can I tell her?'

'Anything which can convince her that Aayush really feels more than what is apparent.'

'Okay, I'll try,' Saumya happily agreed.

* * * * *

On the night before the D-day, I said to Aayush, 'Hey

Aayush, I have an idea.'

'What is it?'

'Saumya and Meenakshi, they always make a fool of you.'

'Yeah, they do it every single moment.'

'Tomorrow is April Fool's day and...no, leave it. You won't be able to do it,' I said with a tinge of sarcasm.

'What? C'mon Anshul, tell me. I am eager to settle scores.'

'Okay, if you insist, then listen. You have to propose to Saniya tomorrow.'

'WHAT? But why and how will this affect Saumya and Meenakshi?'

'Because Saniya is their friend and since you are already involved with Aarti, it will make them livid. And yeah, before proposing to Saniya, you have to tell about your new-found love to Saumya and Meenakshi. No matter what they say, you just stick to the plan.'

'Okay, if you say so. And one more question – when will you stop harassing me sexually?'

'Well, let me think. I think, NEVER,' and my eyes gleamed.

* * * * *

'Here is the letter,' Meenakshi said handing me a letter in the morning.

I was totally amazed at the letter which was written in the same handwriting as that of Aayush.

'See, as I told you, is she not brilliant?' Saumya teased me with pride.

'Okay, okay, now don't try to act so smug. Have you done what I had asked you to do?'

'Yeah, since the last two days I am constantly pestering Saniya and I have also asked her not to discuss it with Deepti.'

'Why?'

'She might sniff the plan, dude.'

'So, now you also agree that she is a bitch,' I smirked.

'ANSHUL!!' Saumya glared at me.

'You just now told me that she could *sniff*. Anyways, I also have some good news for you guys.'

'What?' Meenakshi asked.

'I have convinced Aayush to propose to Saniya but before that, he will inform you about this and you have to react very strongly against it.'

'But why did you tell him this?' asked a shocked Meenakshi.

'Just to make the game more interesting.'

'Aren't you thinking about making us a *bakra* also?'

'Well let's see, I mean, that is also a good idea but not this time. We will do it some other time, baby.'

'Saumya, look, he is again playing games with us,' Meenakshi cringed.

'No, he won't,' Saumya gave me her vote of confidence.

'See, I won't,' I clasped Saumya's hand tightly.

'Okay, Aayush is coming. Meenakshi come with me and take that letter also.'

'And me?'

'You stay here with Aayush. He will definitely tell you.'

'But I want to come too.'

'Saumya, try to understand, we also have to plant the letter. Look, Aayush has to be in the classroom for some time when there is nobody, so that Saniya knows that it is Aayush who placed the letter himself and also it is necessary for her to find it before Aayush officially proposes to her. So try to make him spill the beans to you as soon as possible and then leave him alone in the class for five to six minutes so that we can take the next step.'

'Okay, but come soon.'

* * * * *

'WHAT? ARE YOU OUT OF YOUR MIND?' I heard Saumya shout at the top of her voice.

'But I really like her.'

'AND WHAT ABOUT AARTI?'

'What about her? I will explain to her.'

'What you will explain to her or anyone for that matter is not my problem. But when will you get over this habit of having affairs?'

'Okay, it's time when Saumya will leave him in the class,' I said to Meenakshi, waiting outside the class. 'Here she comes.'

'I told him that I am going to have some water. Till then, let him realise that he is wide off the mark,' Saumya said, coming out of the class.

'Good, now I will follow you in the class and Meenakshi, you can go and take Saniya away exactly fifteen minutes later. At that time none of us will be in the class. Then you have to make Saniya look into her bag. Okay?' I said.

'I have heard you. All the best.'

* * * * *

'Hey Anshul, look what Aayush is saying. He is saying that he is in love with Saniya,' Saumya complained to me as I entered the class.

'He already knows that.'

'You knew it?' Saumya faked amazement.

'Yeah, he told me a few days ago and why are you all over-reacting. Let Saniya decide what she wants to do,' I said calmly.

'Okay, let her come,' Saumya said resignedly.

'By the way, where is she?' Aayush asked.

'She went to the canteen with Meenakshi,' I said.

* * * * *

'How was my acting?' Aayush asked excitedly.

'It was perfect. Now just wait till this news reaches Meenakshi.'

'But what if they tell this to Saniya before I am able to talk to her?'

'Don't worry, I will take care of that. They won't tell her,' I said, trying to curb my laughter.

* * * * *

'Hi Saniya,' I greeted joyfully.

'May I know why someone is ignoring me since the last two days?'

'You are talking about me? Oh sorry partner, I was a little bit busy, but now I am completely at your service, ma'am.'

'That is better. Now where the hell have Saumya and Meenakshi gone?'

'So, someone is feeling bored in my company? And it's me who is accused that I don't have any time to spare.'

'No Anshul, it's not like that.'

'Hey I am feeling hungry. What have you got for lunch?' Meenakshi asked.

'I don't know. Let's go and check. You are coming or not?' Saniya asked, looking at me.

'I have to get my book from the class. You guys go ahead and I will join in a minute,' I said.

So far so good – the plan was going smoothly. They went inside the class. I positioned myself at a far enough corner outside the class from where I could get a part view of the class. Saniya opened her bag and when she turned towards Meenakshi, a piece of paper was visible in her hands.

'What's that?'

'I don't know. I found it in my bag.'

'Open it.'

'Oh crap, this is Aayush's handwriting,' Saniya exclaimed the moment she opened it.

Hi Saniya,

When you will read this, just don't be angry with me or feel bad about it. This is the first time I am writing something like this to someone.

Saniya, as you already know, how much I like you and your personality but I have never told you one thing and that is I like your nature even more. I don't know since when flirting and chatting with you became the only thing that I could enjoy in my whole day. I can never forget that night (you know which one I am talking about). I wanted to say this to you since the last many days and you might have felt also that you had become very special for me, not just because we are good friends but because you are very understanding, cute, emotional and not to forget, very s___ (sorry, yaar*). I know that you already know about Aarti and me. I don't know why I am saying all these things to you; may be because I have not found a better girl than you. I have not told this thing to even my closest friends just because* *they are your best friends also. Only Vineet knows about all this. I even asked him to convey my feelings to you but he never took me seriously.*

I am really very scared because I don't know how will you react, but I don't want to keep my feelings only to myself and I also don't want to lose a good friend like you. Even if you feel otherwise, please don't leave me and if possible, keep this thing between us only. I hope you will understand.

Your friend,

Aayush

Saniya looked at Meenakshi after reading it twice. I entered the room precisely at that moment.

'Anshul, look what I found in my bag.'

I took a heavy breath after reading the letter.

'What is this?'

'Only you can tell. What's going on partner?' I said sarcastically.

'Anshul, I swear I never thought about him like this.'

'Then how did he muster the courage to write this crap? Without a girl's encouragement, nobody can do these things and by the way, which night is he talking about?'

'Anshul really, it's nothing. A few days back we talked on the phone for about an hour.'

'And at precisely what time?'

'Around 2.'

'Wow, around 2 in the night is nothing for you and what exactly did you talk about?'

'Well he was, as usual, flirting with me and I responded in somewhat the same manner.'

'That means you also flirted with him. I can't believe this, I just can't. You know that he is going around with Aarti and still… Saniya, I think we share a better relationship than you two but I never flirted with you and you flirted with him even though you have barely known him for long.'

'Sorry Anshul, tell me what should I do now?' Saniya was almost in tears.

'I don't know,' I said angrily.

'Saumya, look what I have got in my bag,' Saniya said to Saumya on entering the class.

She read it with proper astonishment marks at the right places as if she was reading it for the first time.

'I think you should slap him,' Meenakshi finally said after a short pause.

'No, I think you should wait for him. He might tell you in person or he will want to know your answer. So just hold on,' Saumya suggested.

'I think Saumya is right. And anyways, you two are good friends; don't ruin your friendship over this silly thing. This thing can be solved if you two talk out a bit,' I suggested.

'Hey what happened? Why are you all so serious?' Deepti entered the class.

Saniya leapt across the benches to reach her. We looked at each other. Deepti and Saniya were finally getting together after their nasty fight, but still we didn't want Deepti to intervene until the final scene.

'This is downright absurd and the height of lecherous behaviour,' Deepti croaked in her shrill voice.

Deepti came just at the right time in the picture as we needed a genuine person who could say things which we couldn't and which Deepti did by calling him names.

'I think Deepti is correct. You should sternly handle this matter. Show him that you cannot be swayed by these kinds of tricks,' I seconded Deepti.

'He is such a rascal,' Meenakshi muttered under her breath.

'Shut up, Meenakshi. This is so much fun. Now we have three *bakras* instead of two,' Saumya whispered.

'Just hope that Eashaan wouldn't come to know all this before the secret is divulged, otherwise we all will be the *bakras* instead of them,' Meenakshi said.

* * * * *

'Hi Saniya,' Aayush greeted.

'Hi,' Saniya replied awkwardly. They stood near the stairs outside the class. I had informed Aayush that I had already hinted to Saniya about what he was going to say.

'Saniya, I want to tell you something.'

'I already know what you want to say.'

'Really then, what do you think? Look Saniya, I think we share something more than a friendship. I think you and I look great together.'

'But Aayush, how can you say this to me and what about Aarti? How would she feel when she comes to know all this?'

'Don't worry about that. I will take care of that. But I really like you.'

Saumya, Meenakshi and I stood at a distance, looking at their reactions and Deepti looked tense, sitting on the stairs and constantly staring at them.

'It's been twenty minutes since they have been talking. Should we tell them?' Saumya said.

'Let me go and check,' I said and moved towards the love birds. 'Hello, sorry to disturb you but may I know what is it that you both are talking about?'

'You know it,' Saniya said complacently.

'I have news for you both, so can we go there as it is too much of noise in here. Deepti come on, why are sitting all alone?' I said sensing the intensity with which Saniya was talking to Aayush.

* * * * *

'Aayush, Saniya and Deepti, the three S's (asses), you are nominated for the awards which we have decided to give every year, from now on, on this auspicious day of first April.'

The three looked at the three of us in astonishment.

'Well, don't be so amazed, guys. The '*Bakra* of the Year' award goes to Mr Aayush for his marvellous performance today,' I announced.

A roar of laughter erupted in the air as the five of us, except for Aayush, started to roll on the floor with laughter.

'The next award will be announced by Ms. Saumya,' I passed the baton to Saumya.

'The '*Bakri* of the Year' award goes to Ms. Saniya for her stunning performance today.' The sound of applause grew louder from the rest of the five except for Saniya this time.

'And last but not the least, the award for the 'Best Villainous *Bakri* of the Year' goes to Deepti,' Meenakshi said amidst a round of applause.

'But how did I become April Fool just because I proposed to her?' Aayush asked.

'Not because you had proposed to her but because you gave her a love letter,' I smiled.

'But if he wrote that letter it means he already knew about the plan. Right?' Saniya asked.

'Excuse me, what letter? Saniya mentioned some letter to

me,' said a baffled Aayush.

'Saniya, he doesn't know about the letter,' I told Saniya.

'Would anyone tell me what letter are we talking about?' Aayush almost yelled.

'Okay, okay, here is the letter,' Saumya handed him the letter.

'Whoa! This is my writing, man. But I didn't write this letter,' Aayush exclaimed.

'Then who wrote it? You?' Saniya looked at us.

'Not me, it was Meenakshi,' I said pointing at Meenakshi.

'Amazing *yaar*, it is so very good; just exactly like Aayush's handwriting,' Deepti said, looking at the letter.

'The mastermind behind this whole story is Anshul. We had planned that first Saumya would tell Saniya that Aayush considered her more than a friend. Then we put this letter in Saniya's bag and made her believe that it had been done by Aayush and which was not difficult. Then Anshul convinced Aayush that he could take revenge against Saumya and me by making us a *bakra* today if he proposed to Saniya. Incidentally he didn't know that we were just putting on the act of being angry. When Saniya found the letter, fortunately Deepti came into the picture which was not planned but was extremely crucial because we required someone who could corroborate that it was a serious matter and that Saniya should at least scold Aayush for writing this. So when Aayush went to propose to Saniya, the stage was already set. The only thing we feared was that Saniya might slap him, considering Saniya's past record,' Meenakshi said, grinning from ear to ear.

'So the moral of the story is "He who digs a hole for others, finally goes down into the drain himself." Aayush wanted to make a fool of others but he didn't know that the real *bakra* was he himself from the very beginning,' I concluded. Aayush glared at me.

'Oh no *yaar*, I was so happy that I got the first love letter of my life and you guys ruined the moment.'

'Oh, my poor friend,' Saumya patted Saniya's back.

'You know what? I suspected that it was some kind of a plan but I didn't say anything,' Deepti said after a long time.

'Oh right!' I said.

'No really,' Deepti defended herself.

'Okay, okay, cut it out. I have my camera with me to make this moment more special,' Saumya said. 'Say *Happy Bakra Divas*.'

Someone had rightly said that "pictures fade but memories don't."

20

The Last Kiss

I somehow didn't feel great as I should have. A sort of unhappiness engulfed me. This was my college, which we all had called a jail in which the warden was the jailor. But now it had been my home for four years. Suddenly I felt as though I was struck by a lightning bolt. I was going to leave this college in a few days. Tears welled up in my eyes at the mere thought of leaving college and all my friends, especially Saumya for an unwarranted journey into the real world which everyone says is as brutal as it can be.

I had absolutely no idea why I felt weakness in my limbs. The thought of saying goodbye to the campus, the grass, the flowers, the benches, the classrooms, the building, the library, the faculty and even the college gate, which had become a special part of my existence, made a lump arise in my throat.

College was about to end and I didn't know what to do. I didn't want to leave this place. Was I afraid of the outside world or was it that my love for college, which I never knew existed in me, was making me depressed? I just wanted to live the moment, only the moment and nothing else.

I remembered all those silly fights with Avantika, Shyam, Vineet, Aayush, Meenakshi, Shubh and even Saumya. After a few days, after we left this place, we might not ever meet again.

'Anshul, we joined college not to achieve only something but to make ourselves capable to achieve everything in life. So just savour this moment and stop feeling miserable,' Saumya said, caressing my hand.

I looked at her face. It was glowing like a pearl. I felt a feeling of contentment creep inside my body.

* * * * *

Everyone was excited about the farewell party which was scheduled to take place two days later. No stones had been left unturned by the girls in the quest of looking the best. I felt the girls took so much care of themselves for only two reasons – firstly, no girl wanted to look inferior to any other and secondly, each wanted to put on so much makeup that we, the boys, would admire them and compliment them. How else should it matter as to who is looking prettier or not?

The boys too did not want to be left behind. Many had decided to shave and have a bath that day after a long time. Clothes were exchanged between each other and utmost care was taken to find a guy from some other branch so that the girls wouldn't find any connection. How else could they arrange for new clothes at such a short notice?

'I am wearing a pink saree that day. What are you wearing?' Saumya told me cheerfully about her plans.

'I don't know. I have not thought about it,' I smiled.

'Why? It is an important day.'

'For me, spending time with you is more important and that I have planned already.'

'Oh my *koochie-koo*, my *sona*, my baby, I love you baby,' she tickled me.

'Saumya don't; just don't do it,' I said trying to escape from her vicious hands.

'Anshul, can I talk to you for a minute?' Deepti said.

'Yeah, okay. Why don't you come here?' I suggested apprehensively.

'Don't worry. I will go for a walk with Meenakshi and Saniya. You guys can carry on,' Saumya offered.

'Thanks Saumya,' Deepti said.

'Yeah, what do you want to talk about?'

'Anshul, I know what you think about me, but I just wanted to tell you that I am not as bad as you think I am.'

'How do you know what I think about you?'

'I know it. You know girls have this special ability to read the mind, which you can call the sixth sense.'

'Deepti, let me make one thing very clear. I am not a judge of anyone's character and that's why I don't want to judge you on the basis of your relationship with Eashaan or now with Vineet. Since I don't know your side of the story in either case, it is not possible for me to act as an arbitrator.'

'Thanks Anshul. I knew you would understand me.'

'Deepti, sorry to disappoint you but I didn't say that I understand you. It would have been better if you hadn't asked me about my views about you.'

'But if I say that I want to know?'

'Then I would say, you are wasting your time.'

'Anshul, I consider you as my one of my good friends

and I can expect you to tell me what you feel about me,' Deepti said as I simpered.

'Deepti, don't try this thing with me. My emotional quotient is very low.'

'I know Anshul that you are very practical and that's why I think only you can understand me. If you still don't want to tell me what you think about me, then it's fine with me.'

I grinned again. 'Since you want to hear it, then I will tell you. I think you are very intelligent academically, but you are not as devoted towards your friends like Saniya as they are towards you. I think you are a bit selfish, but then that is my view. I consider you a greedy and money-minded person because of some of your acts in the past. But that is only my point of view. For Saniya, you are a gem of a friend and that is exactly why you both are together again. Now it is up to you to prove her right or wrong and since you behaved wrongly towards her once, I would appreciate it if there was to be no second time, ' I said calmly.

She kept looking at me for any sigh of rage or anger on my face.

'Thanks, Anshul for conveying your true feelings. You know I considered you as a....'

'Deepti, sorry, but I didn't ask you for your opinion about me. So it would be better if we didn't discuss it any further.'

'Okay, as you wish. Anyways, I wanted to tell you that Vineet and I have liked each other from the very beginning. It was Eashaan who came in between us and as the things turned out, Vineet didn't have the chance to express his feelings for me.'

'If you liked Vineet from the beginning, then why didn't

you tell Eashaan initially itself that you liked someone else? Why did you keep him in the lurch?'

'I thought that he would understand as time passed.'

'You know what, Deepti? I know that Vineet loves you more than anyone in this world. Although we don't talk much nowadays, I have always felt that his love for you is unconditional and his devotion to Shubh and Eashaan is unparallel in every sense. I know, in love, we don't care about many things, so it is sort of okay with me. Anyways, anything else you want to discuss?' I smiled again.

'Anshul, I know that Vineet loves me a lot.'

'And you? What about you?'

'I also love him and that's why we are together.'

'How can I comment on that? This question you have to ask yourself. But still one question is in my mind.'

'What is that?'

'Why in the blue moon are you explaining this to me? What do you want me to do?'

'Nothing; I just thought that you could tell Saumya and Meenakshi about what I was going through.'

'Well, obviously I will tell Saumya what we have talked about but if you are thinking that I will act as a mediator between you and them, then I am sorry I can't help you. I don't advise her or anybody in taking decisions, until it is the only way left. And the same is with Meenakshi. I don't tell her what to do in her personal life.'

'I am not asking you to mediate but at least they will know my side of the story.'

'Why don't you tell them yourself?'

'I am afraid they won't listen to me.'

'Okay, then I will try but I can't promise anything. I

have to go now,' I said and stood up.

'Okay....thanks for listening.'

'Hey, did Vineet know that you had come to talk about all this to me?'

'No, he doesn't know.'

'Okay then, 'bye,' I said and left.

* * * * *

'You are looking good,' Aayush complimented me.

'Thanks to the shirt you gave me,' I said.

'When are they reaching here?'

'I don't know. They were in Saniya's car when I called them.'

'So what should we do till then?'

'Let's watch the movie we left yesterday.'

* * * * *

'Where are you? I am waiting in the auditorium,' Saumya called me.

'We are just coming,' I said and hung up.

The three of them were seated in the last row. Meenakshi waved at us. She was looking strikingly different in a saree. Saniya was wearing an orange *lehenga*.

'Where is Saumya?' I asked.

'She is just coming from the restroom. There she is.'

Aayush and I looked at the door. A girl in pink saree appeared. She looked stunningly gorgeous and her hair waved like a stream.

'Hey, who is that?' I asked Aayush. 'I think I have seen her somewhere,' I said with a smile.

The light in the background was obstructing our view.

That figure came closer to us.

'Hi Saumya,' Aayush said, obviously stunned.

'Hi! You both are always late,' she said and came and sat next to me.

'Will you marry me?' I whispered in her ear.

'What? Why this question now?'

'Just answer me.'

'Yes, of course.'

'Okay, then let's go.'

'Where?'

'Some temple or may be the court.'

'Stop kidding, Anshul.'

'I am not kidding. You are looking so stunning today. I think I am in love again. Where was this beauty hidden all this time?'

Saumya blushed. I looked at her face with the desire to kiss her.

'How come I have never kissed you till now?' I asked.

Saumya was now finding it very difficult to hide her red face from Meenakshi and Saniya.

'Are you blushing?' Saniya asked. 'Hey partner, what did you tell her?'

'Nothing, I just asked her why we hadn't kissed till now.'

Saumya looked at me with disbelief.

'What, you have not kissed each other till now?' Saniya looked at me incredulously.

'As if you have done it a lot of times,' I said.

'You never know,' Saniya winked at me.

'Eashaan is coming here. So I should ask him whether what you are saying is true or not.'

'I didn't say anything and don't utter a word in front of

him, else I will kill you with my own hands.'

'Oh, so you are threatening me? EASHAAN,' I called out his name aloud.

'Oh please partner, sorry *yaar*.'

'That's better,' I waved at Eashaan.

'DOG,' Saniya said.

'You said something?'

'No, nothing. Okay guys, I will catch you later.'

* * * * *

'Hey I am coming in a minute,' I said lovingly.

'Where are you going?' Saumya asked with a bit of a fret in her voice.

'Just coming, *babu.* Don't worry, I will be back in a minute.'

As I was leaving the auditorium, I saw Deepti and Vineet enter the auditorium as they went to sit at the other corner.

* * * * *

'Where are Saumya and Aayush?' I asked Meenakshi who was sitting alone in the auditorium.

'I don't know. Aayush wanted to tell something to Saumya.'

'Okay, so what's going on?'

'Nothing. Just thinking a lot these days.'

'And what exactly are you thinking about?'

'About people and their traits.'

'Okay, so you are thinking about Deepti and me.'

'I didn't say that.'

'Did I tell you that I have the special ability to read the mind, especially of girls?'

'So then, you must know what I was thinking?'

'Yeah, sort of. For example, you were thinking that how come we never shared more than a cordial relationship all these years, but now you think that since you have missed the bus, so what options do you have now? Am I correct?'

'How do you know that?' she was amazed.

'And apart from that, you are also thinking or rather cursing yourself for calling Deepti your best friend when she is not even worthy of entering your house.'

Meenakshi looked at me with utter amazement.

I smiled and thanked Saumya for telling me all about these things and many others which Meenakshi had told her.

'So you must know the solution also?'

'Sorry, I don't know the solution but I know one thing for sure and it is that you have to solve this problem and many others on your own,' I said smilingly.

'Is something serious going on?' Saumya asked, coming with Aayush from behind.

'Nothing special. Meenakshi was just telling me how much she loves me,' I said.

'Really Meenakshi!' Saumya also smiled.

'Yeah, I was just telling him how he had ignored my feelings and broken my heart when he asked you out,' Meenakshi said animatedly.

'So where have you been?' I asked Saumya as she sat beside me.

'I will tell you later.'

* * * * *

'GUYS IT'S TME TO PARTY. COME ON TO THE DANCE FLOOR,' somebody announced to draw our attention as we sat on grass. The dance floor was set in the open.

'Let's go,' Aayush said to us.

'Take them; I am not coming,' I said backing off.

'I am coming,' Meenakshi said.

'I am also staying here.'

'Okay, let's go,' Aayush said.

'Aayush proposed to me today,' Saumya said as we watched Aayush and Meenakshi go towards the dance floor. The music grew louder. I looked at Saumya and then at Aayush again.

'He said that he wanted to tell this since many days but now when only a few days are left, it is now or never.'

I felt betrayed. A wave of anger surged inside my chest.

'And what did you say?' I asked, forcing a smile on my face.

'I said what I needed to say in this situation. He was almost in tears when he told me all this. I told him that I only loved one person and he knew him very well.'

I kept quiet.

'Saumya, how many people are there right now?'

'Almost everyone from the final year and third year, but why are you asking?'

'Give me a number.'

'May be around six hundred or more.'

'Okay, close your eyes.'

'But why?'

'Just close them,' I held her hand as she closed her beautiful large eyes.

I looked around. Everyone was dancing or was busy with each other and I KISSED SAUMYA. She opened her eyes just to find my face very close to her. Our bodies were so close that I could feel her heavy breathing mix with mine. She closed her eyes. I caressed her silky hair and the fragrance of her body made me go absolutely weak in my knees. We kissed for exactly thirty-five seconds and those thirty-five seconds were the best thirty-five seconds of my whole life till that day which consisted of more than seventy-seven hundred days. When it was over, I wanted to do it again and again every day for the rest of my life. I bent down on my knees in front of those six hundred pairs of eyes which were now transfixed on us.

'Will you marry me?' I asked Saumya.

Tears welled in her eyes from nowhere. She was looking at me with only love and nothing else.

'Yes my *paglu,* I will.'

Epilogue

Looking at the past from the sidelines is both enthralling and unsatisfying because memories are like a mirror with so many reflections watching you at one time. But at the same time, you can't live again those moments to rectify your mistakes or to improvise your success.

It's been almost two years since the college got over but still the reminiscences of our college days (glorious or inglorious, I don't know) are still fresh in our minds. We all have taken different routes in our lives after college.

Eashaan has started taking care of his father's business but soon got fed up with the daily accounting and customer handling. Now he is working as a software consultant with an MNC. Saniya also works in the same city but in a different company. And by the way, Saniya accepted Eashaan's proposal on her twenty-third birthday last year and now they are planning to get married, I think maybe next year.

Vineet is working in a bank as a junior manager, in Pune while Deepti is working at Indore as an assistant or consultant. And they both are also getting married soon.

Avantika finally accepted Shubh's proposal and now the real task is to convince each other's parents about their love. Well, the good news is that they both work in the same office but they still have a long way to go.

Now who else is left? Oh...h...h...hh yes, Aayush and Aarti. They both parted ways only to find that they were walking on the crossroads of life. After numerous break-ups and the same number of reunions, finally they have again broken up. I mean don't take it personally, guys. I think that you both should be married in your next reunion so that we can be sure that we don't have to take care of the number of your reunions/breakups.

Finally, about Saumya and me, well...after college, her father won the last battle, and hence the war, when he managed to stop Saumya from joining the company. That's life, I guess. Now she is married to a businessman and they both have a baby boy, whose name coincidentally is Anshul. And what I am doing? I am trying to live with the absence of her smile, her nonsensical chatter and her touch. Now her absence is the one thing that I can't manage to fill but what I can do is to make her memories more memorable by respecting her decision.

Enough about me; now go and give some rest to your eyes which might me paining because mine are. So goodnight, asta-la-vista, *Baby (gosh, I wanted to say this for so long) and* khuda-haafiz *till our next meeting.*

Love, Life and Ambition

By Bharat Agarwal

Price	:	Rs. 99
Pages	:	240
Size	:	5.0×7.75 inches
Binding	:	Paperback
Language	:	English
Subject	:	Fiction/Romance
ISBN	:	9788183520102

About the book:

As a young schoolboy, Ayushman joins Scindia School in Gwalior and in no time he becomes the best student in school and icon for all.

The school ambience helps him to devote his full time to his work, and teachers always boosts him in his aim, which is to unveil Albert Einstein's Theory of Relativity, $E=mc^2$. At Scindia, his sweet classmate falls in love with him and she keeps trying to get her lascivious desires fulfilled. Similarly, Ayushman's attention too gets diverted when he sees an alluring girl by his side in a science fair, and later she becomes his devastating desire. With $E=mc^2$, love always goes parallel in their lives, though none of them knows anything about anyone's heart since the very inception of this book. What eye doesn't see and what mind doesn't know, this book has it all.

Ayushman's desire to become a next sapient Albert Einstein always has different faces. Sometimes his spirits soaring and at the other times plummeting deep below, but he always continues to strive till he brings $E=mc^2$ nearer to its final destination. After all he has to become Einstein II.

But, is it possible for someone to be next Albert Einstein? Did Albert Einstein himself ever fell in love as Ayushman? Does ever love and science go hand-in-hand?

To find out the final result, the novel has to be read as this unsaid story ends on a most unpredictable note.